Martha C. Thomas

Sir Gawayne and the Green Knight

A comparison with the French Perceval

Martha C. Thomas

Sir Gawayne and the Green Knight
A comparison with the French Perceval

ISBN/EAN: 9783337298869

Printed in Europe, USA, Canada, Australia, Japan

Cover: Foto ©Andreas Hilbeck / pixelio.de

More available books at **www.hansebooks.com**

SIR GAWAYNE

AND THE

GREEN KNIGHT

A COMPARISON WITH THE FRENCH PERCEVAL

PRECEDED BY

AN INVESTIGATION OF THE AUTHOR'S OTHER·WORKS

AND FOLLOWED BY

A CHARACTERIZATION OF GAWAIN

IN ENGLISH POEMS

———∞———

INAUGURAL DISSERTATION

FOR OBTAINING THE DEGREE OF DOCTOR OF PHILOSOPHY

PRESENTED BEFORE THE PHILOSOPHICAL FACULTY

OF THE

UNIVERSITY OF ZÜRICH

BY

MARTHA CAREY THOMAS

———✳———

ZÜRICH

PRINTED BY ORELL FÜSSLI & CO.

1883.

I.

An investigation of the author's other poems:—

II.

III.

Sir Gawain in English poems:—

"Sir Gawayne and the Green Knight" was published for the first time in Sir Fred. Madden's "Syr Gawayne, a collection of ancient romance-poems by Scotish and English authors, relating to that celebrated knight of the Round Table. London 1839. Printed for the Bannatyne Club". Prefixed to this edition is a description of the unique MS. Cott. Nero A x; in the same portion of which, and directly preceding our Sir Gawayne, are three other poems, written in the same hand and all (Madden ibid. p. 301) "most unquestionably composed by the author of the romance".

Morris edited these three poems, under the titles of the Pearl, Cleanness, and Patience, for the E. E. T. S., in 1864 (2nd ed. 1869): and in the same year, for the same society, reedited Sir Gawayne and the Green Knight (2nd ed. likewise 1869). He agrees with Madden in attributing all four poems to one and the same author; alleging for his opinion similarity of dialect.

Prof. Trautmann in his Habilitationssft. Leipzig 1876, "Über Verfasser und Entstehungszeit einiger allit. Gdte. des Altengl." agrees with Morris, while deeming insufficient the ground assigned by him for his opinion. He himself reaches the same conclusion by applying "the best tests we can have" — those of *wort- und phrasen-gebrauch und versbau*. The Pearl, not being written in alliteration, falls without the limits of his subject. But in his article "Der Dichter Huchown und seine Werke" (Anglia I, p. 118—120) he attributes the Pearl to the author of the other three poems, and enumerates the reasons as follows:—

I. 48 words rare or unknown in other poems and common to these 4.

II. The similar treatment of the alliterative rhymes:
   a, the frequent alliteration — wh : w.
   b, the frequent alliteration of the spiritus asper with the spiritus lenis.
   c, such alliterations as *excused: scape, expoune: speche*. He gives two examples from the Pearl.
   d, the frequent alliteration of combinations of 2 and 3 letters with each other (*i. e.* sp, cl, str, etc.), three in a line.

Ground I. is not conclusive, because if we assume (as we have the right to assume, cf. Morris 2nd ed.

of Allit. Poems, preface p. IX, note) another poet writing in precisely the same dialect, he would naturally make use of words which must have been common to that section of the country.

Ground II. does not seem to me *entirely* convincing, because *a* and *ḃ* are peculiarities which the Pearl shares with William of Palerne (cf. Trautmann Üb. Verf. u. Entst. p. 14); and *d* is found not only in Gaw. Cl. and Pat., but also, in a less degree, in Mort Arthure; and, to a much greater extent, in the Alexander Fragments.

Trautmann is satisfied here with much lighter evidence than in the case of the poem of Gawain (cf. Üb. Verf. u. Entst.). Yet, apart from the complete proof he himself brings, there was, as I shall point out later for another purpose, an intimate connection between moral and descriptive passages of Gaw. and Cl.; while between the Pearl and the other poems there is no such link. It is separated from them by its versification; by the blending of allegory and personal feeling; by the different use too of the Bible, insomuch as while Cl. and Pat. are merely founded upon it, the author of the Pearl transports himself into the scenes in Revelations which he describes.

Supplementary proof leading to the conclusion that the Pearl is by the author of Gaw. Cl. and Pat.

From the rhymes of the Pearl no conclusion can be drawn except in so far as their purity speaks for the same author. The only comparison possible is with the 505 rhyming lines in Gaw. The spelling in the poems varies greatly, even where the scribe is controlled by the rhyme (cf. Gaw. 1643 lawe: knowe and Pl. 541 knaw : owe etc.), but the rhymes are remarkably pure. The rule for the different endings ie, y, e (cf. ten Brink Chancer Stud. p. 22 ff.) is observed Gaw. 228 and 247. In the Pl., although mostly regarded, it is sometimes broken — 798 debonerté: felonye; but the instances in Gaw. are too few to enable us to draw any conclusion.

There are however the following similarities of thought and expression between the Pl. and the other poems.

Pl. 341—348 may be compared with Pat. 5—8; and especially Pl. *l.* 344 :—

· "Who nedeȝ schal pole be not so pro."
with Pat. 6 :—

"And quo for pro may noȝt pole, þe pikker he
⌊suffers."

The prominence given to the Virgin Pl. 423
—36 .... 453—56 may be compared with
Cl. 1069—1084.

The "pearl" is not only the symbol for the
poet's lost child, but occurs in manifold combinations;
on the breasts and garments of the 100,000 virgins,
in their crowns, in the border of his child's robes
etc., and is everywhere apostrophized and praised.
We may therefore expect to find some trace of this
in the other poems. Compare Gaw. 2364—5:

"As *perle* bi þe quite pese is of prys more,
So is Gawayn, in god fayth, bi oper gay knyȝteȝ."

Cl. 1068:—

"Þat euer is polyced als playn as þe *perle* seluen."

Cl. 556:—

"With-outen maskle oper mote as margerye *perle*."

(Cf. Pl. 199 "myryeste margarys").

Cl. 1116—1132:—

"And pure þe with penaunce tyl þou a perle worþe.
Perle praysed is prys, þer perre is schewed,
Þaȝ hym not derrest be demed to dele for penies,
Quat may þe cause be called, bot for hir clene hwes,
Þat wynnes worschyp, abof alle whyte stones?
For ho schynes so schyr þat is of *schap rounde*,
Wyth-outen *faut oper fylþe ȝif* ho fyn were."

etc.

Cf. Pl. 1 ff. symbolically of his child:—

> "Perle plesaunte to prynces paye,
> To clanly clos in golde so clere,
> Oute of oryent I hardyly saye,
> Ne proued I neuer her precios pere,
> *So rounde*, so reken in vche araye,
> So smal, *so smope* her sydeʒ were."

and Pl. 737:—

> "For hit (the pearl) is wemleʒ, clene & clere,
> And *endeleʒ rounde* & blype of mode."

Ten Brink (p. 438) has remarked that the Pearl begins and closes with the same words; the same rather unusual device is found also in the other poems. Pat. opens:—

> "Patience is a poynt, paʒ hit displese ofte."

and closes, 531:—

> "Þat pacience is a nobel poynt, paʒ hit displese ofte.
> Amen."

Gaw. begins with an account of the landing of Brutus in England after the fall of Troy, *l*. 1:—

> "Siþen þe sege & þe assaut watʒ sesed at Troye."

l. 13:—

> "And fer ouer þe French flod Felix Brutus
> On mony bonkkes ful brode Bretayn he setteʒ."

and closes (except for a prayer) *l*. 2524:

> "Sypen Brutus, þe bolde burne, boʒed hider fyrst,
> After þe segge & þe asaute watʒ sesed at Troye,
> I—wysse."

Cleanness opens : —

"Clannesse who-so kyndly cowpe commende."

and closes (except for a prayer) *l.* 1809 : —

"Ande clannes is his comfort, & coyntyse he louyes,
And pose pat seme arn & swete schyn se his face."

Although the verbal likeness is here not so strictly observed as in the Pl., Pat., and Gaw.; yet it is clear that the poet had the opening lines in his mind.

The following similar expressions occur.

Pl. 380 : —
> "stok oper ston."

Compare Cl. 1343, 1523, & 1720 : —
> "stokkes & stones",

Pl. 982 : —
> "Þat schyrrer þen sunne with schafteʒ schon."

Cf. Pat. 455—6 : —

"Þe schyre sunne hit vmbe—schon, paʒ no schafte myʒt
Þe mountaunce of a lyttel mote, vpon pat man schyne."

Pl. 231 : —
> "No gladder gome heþen in to grece."

Cf. Gaw. : —
> "Þe gayest in to Grece."

The two similies Pl. 183 :
> "Wyth yʒen open & mouth ful clos
> I stod as hende as hawk in halle."

and 1085 : —

"I stod as stylle as dased quayle."

recall the lover of knightly sports whom we see in the author of Gaw.

Finally, the author of the Pearl has a mannerism in the use of comparisons: — they appear in clusters of two or more. The same is found in Cl. and Pat., and, to a lesser extent, in Gaw. Thus out of the 35 comparisons in the Pearl 15 occur in groups: — 76. 77. — 114. 115. — 212. 213. — 607. 608. — 801. 802. — 1018. 1025. 1026. — 1112. 1115. —; out of the 24 in Cl., 14: — 222. 223. 226. — 554. 556. — 790. 791. — 1018. 1022. — 1132. 1134. — 1694. 1696. 1·697. —; out of the 7 in Pat., 3: — 268. 272. 274. —; out of the 19 in Gaw., 6: — 235. 236. — 2202. 2203. — 2293, two comparisons—.

We have then no reason to doubt that the Pearl is by the author of Gaw., Cl., and Pat.

The relative dates of the four poems.

Trautmann (Über Verf. u. Entst. p. 33) says: — "Ich bekenne mich ausser stande in diesem punkte

eine auch nur einigermassen wahrscheinliche ent-
scheidung zu treffen."

Ten Brink, on the other hand (Lit. Gesch. p.
435) says:— "den übergang zu den entschieden reli-
giös gefärbten schöpfungen unseres dichters bildet eine
dichtung, welche einen wendepunkt in des mannes
innerem leben nicht blos erschliessen lässt, sondern
unmittelbar darstellt. Mit recht führt sie den namen
'Die Perle'". That is to say, he places the Pearl
between Gawain and the other two poems; apparently
between Gawain and Cleanness, because, p. 439, he
finds in Patience not only the greatest poetic per-
fection but evidence that the poet himself was then
growing old in poverty and solitude. This is the same
method applied by Prof. ten Brink to Kynewulf:
but the evidence is here less convincing. At least I
have not been able to discover in the Pearl any of
the characteristics of a turning point; and again in
the four poems which lie before us there is no such
striking dissimilarity as would lead us to assume
any such turning point. I prefer in defending the
latter assertion to use some of Prof. ten Brink's own
phrases. — "Diese ganze kunst endlich *(in Gawain)*
steht im dienste sittlicher ideen. Man mag es tadeln,
dass unser dichter das *Hæc fabula docet* gar zu

deutlich ausspricht." "Zwei ideen namentlich finden in der Perle ausdruck, beide, wenn auch nicht mit gleicher entschiedenheit, bereits in Gawein dargestellt: die ideen der unschuld (reinheit) und der ergebung in den göttlichen willen. Jede derselben machte der dichter später zum gegenstand eines besondern werkes: Clannesse und Pacience." "Das subjective element aber, das in der Perle so mächtig ist, macht sich hier (in Cleanness and Patience) nur gelegentlich geltend....... Auf objective darstellung ist hier wie in Gawein das augenmerk des dichters gerichtet."

Would it be supposed, from the above passages that a cleft divided Gawain from Cleanness and Patience? Would it not rather be thought that they belonged together while the Pearl stood apart? We are expressly assured that Gawain is not distinguished from the other poems by a difference in the "inner life" of the poet. Therefore if the Pearl, falling between Gaw. and Cl., in any way represent a turning-point or a transition, it must have been that the poet at this time resolved to forsake all but sacred subjects. In the whole Pearl however there is no trace of such a resolve, no remorse for the past, no purpose to lead a new life, and yet the resolve would have been an austere one, made by a man of whom ten

Brink pertinently says:— "wenn er nun nicht ein didakter oder allegoriker, wie hundert andere unter seinen zeitgenossen geworden ist, so beruht das darauf, dass er in seiner dichterischen intuition in natur und leben eine tiefe symbolik erkannte."

On the other hand, there is an intimate connection between Gawain and Cleanness: — a similarity of moral, as of special passages, greater than exists else where among the four poems; and the Pearl, if we assume it to lie between them, appears less in the light of a transition from the one to the other, than in that of an interruption, after which the old style and the old chain of thought are resumed. The points of contact between Gawain and Cleanness are as follows.

There is a general resemblance between the description of the seasons from New Year to New Year in Gaw., and a passage in Cl. to which, although it is a paraphrase of Genesis VIII, 22, the poet has given his own colouring, cf. Gaw. 500—530 and Cl. 523—527, especially Gaw. 529—:

"And þus ȝirneȝ þe ȝere in ȝisterdays mony."

with Cl. 527:—

"Bot euer renne restleȝ rengneȝ ȝe per-inne."

Gaw. 72—73:—

"When þay had waschen, worþyly þay wenten to sete,
Þe best burne ay abof, as hit best semed."

Cf. Cl. 91—92:—

„Ful manerly with marchal mad forto sitte,
As he watȝ dere of de-gre dressed his seete,"

and Cl. 114—115:—

"Ay þe best byfore & bryȝtest atyred
Þe derrest at þe hyȝe dese þat dubbed wer fayrest."

Gaw. 482—484:—

"& kene men hem *serued,*
Of *alle dayntyeȝ double* as derrest myȝt falle,
Wyth alle maner *of mete & mynstralcie* boþe."

Cf. Cl. 120—121:—

"And ȝet þe symplest in þat sale watȝ *serued to*
                                      · [*þe fulle,*
Boþe with menske, & with *mete & mynstralsy* noble."

Gaw. 497:—

"For paȝ men ben *mery* in mynde quen þay han
                              [*mayn drynk*"

and Gaw. 899—900:—

"Þat mon much merþe con make,
For wyn in his hed þat wende."

Cf. Cl. 123:—   ·

"And þay bigonne to be *glad* þat *god drink haden.*"

Gaw. 114—120:—

"Þise *were diȝt on* þe *des,* & derworþly serued,
& siþen mony siker segge *at* þe *sidbordeȝ.*
Þen þe first cors come with *crakkyng of trumpes.*

Wyth mony *baner ful bryȝt* þat per-bi henged,
Nwe *nakryn noyse* with þe noble *pipes*,
Wylde werbles & wyȝt wakned lote,
Þat mony hert ful hiȝe hef at her towches."

and Gaw. 123:—

"Þat pine to fynde þe place þe peple bi-forne
For to sette þe *sylueren*, þat *sere sewes halden.*"

Cf. Cl. 1397—1406:—

"Þenne watȝ alle þe halle flor hiled with knyȝtes,
& *barounes at* þe *side—bordes* bounet ay-where,
For non watȝ *dressed vpon dece bot* þe *dere seluen*,
& his clere concubynes in clopes ful bryȝt.
When alle segges were þer set, þen seruyse bygynnes,
Sturnen *trumpen* strake stuen in halle,
Aywhere by þe wowes wrasten *krakkes*,
& brode *baneres* per-bi *blusnande of gold*;
Burnes *berande* þe *bredes* vpon brode skeles,
Þat were of *sylueren* syȝt seerved per-wyth."

and Cl. 1413:—

"& ay þe *nakeryn noyse*, notes of *pipes.*"

Compare the description of Arthur's Christmas
feast, Gaw. 45—46:—

"With alle þe mete & þe *mirþe* þat men coupe a-vyse;
Such glaumande gle glorious to here."

and Gaw. 50—56:—

"With *alle þe wele of þe worlde* pay woned þer samen,
Þe most *kyd knyȝteȝ* vnder kryste seluen,
& þe *louelokkest ladies* þat euer lif haden,

2

& he þe *comlokest kyng* þat þe court haldes;
For al watȝ þis fayre folk en her *first age*,
oñ sille;
Þe *hapnest vnder heuen.*"

with the description of the sons of Adam before the
Flood, Cl. 252—262:—

"Hit wern þe *fayrest* of forme & of face als,
Þe most & þe *myriest* þat maked wern euer,
Þe *styfest,* þe *stalworþest* þat stod euer on fete;
& lengest lyf in hem lent of ledeȝ alle oþer,
For hit was þe *forme-foster* þat þe folde bred,
Þe apel aunctereȝ suneȝ þat adam watȝ called,
To wham god hade geuen alle þat gayn were,
Alle blysse boute blame þat bodi myȝt have,
& þose lykkest to þe lede þat lyued next after,
For-þy so semly to see syþen wern none."

These are the descriptive passages which have
the greatest likeness to each other in the two poems.
It seems more probable that Gawain was written
first on account of the knightly descriptions which
the author would be more apt to introduce into his
Bible narrative, had he just employed them in place
in his romance. Also the lines in Gaw. have more
of the freshness of an original.

The oneness of moral between the two poems
is even more striking.

Purity and "trawþe" are enforced in *Gawain.*
The covenant Gaw. makes with the Green Knight

to seek him on the next New Year's day,
l. 403 :—

"& þat I swere þe for soþe, & by my seker traweþ"

is a trial of his faithfulness. Gawain's shield bears
a pentangle *l.* 626 :—

"in by토knyng of *trawþe.*"

L. 631 ff. :—

"For-þy hit accordeȝ to þis knyȝt & to his cler armeȝ
For ay faythful in fyue & sere fyue sypeȝ,
Gawan watȝ for gode knawen."

L. 638 :—
"As tulk of tale most *trwe.*"

L. 1091 :—
"Þe segge *trwe.*"

During Gawain's last temptation by the wife of
the Green Knight, when "gret perile bi-twene hem
stod," *l.* 1773—1775 :—

"He cared for his cortaysye lest crapayn he were,
& more for his meschef, ȝif he schulde make synne,
& be *traytor* to þat tolke, þat þat telde aȝt."

Upon seeing Gawain at the appointed place,
the Green Knight says *l.* 2241 :—

"& þou hatȝ tymed þi trauayl as *true mon* schulde."

and further *l.* 2348 ff :—

"& þou *trystyly* þe trawþe & *trwly* me haldeȝ.
Al þe gayne þow me gef, as god mon schulde."

and again *l.* 2353—4 :—

> "*Trwe mon trwe* restore,
> Þenne þar mon drede no waþe."

Gawain accuses himself and says l. 2382 ff. : —

> "Now am I fawty, & falce & ferde haf ben euer;
> Of trecherye & *vn-trawpe* boþe bityde sorȝe
> & care."

Of the eight chief examples of God's punishment given in *Cleanness* 4 are for uncleanness, and 4 for want of "trawpe" (the poet understands under the virtue "trawpe" at once faith [belief], and faithfulness) — the fall of the angels, the disobedience of Lot's wife, the taking of Jerusalem and the punishment of Nebuchadnezzar.

L. 208 :—

> "& he (Satan) vnkyndely as a karle ky*dde areward*."

Lot's wife is described *l.* 979 :—

> "Bot þe balleful burde, þat neuer bode keped."

She was turned into a pilar of salt *l,* 996 :—

> "For two fautes þat þe fol watȝ founde in *mistraupe.*"

The cause of the captivity of the Jews is given *l.* 1161 ff. :—

> "For þat folke in her fayth watȝ founden *vntrwe,*
> Þat haden hyȝt þe hyȝe god to halde of hym euer."

Line 235—236 :—

> "Hit (the fall of man) lyȝt
> Þurȝ þe faut of a freke þat fayled in *trawpe.*".

The cleanness (by which our poet understands preëminently chastity) of Gawain, cf. *l.* 653: — "his clannes & his cortaysye croked were neuer," is abundantly emphasized by his triumphantly withstanding the temptations of the wife of the Green Knight. The Green Knight says *l.* 2362—3:—

"I sende hir to asay þe, & soþly me pynkkeȝ, On þe fautlest freke, þat euer on fote ȝede."

Further on he points the moral *l.* 2366—2368:—

"Bot here yow lakked a lyttel, sir, & lewte yow wonted, Bot þat watȝ no *wylyde werke* ne *wowyng nauper*, Bot for ȝe lufed your lyf, þe lasse I yow blame."

and again 2391:—

"Þou art confessed so clene, be-knowen of þy mysses."

In Cleanness, as its name shows, "cleanness" is the chief moral enforced, yet the special moral (cf. Gaw. 2368) is also drawn, Cl. *l.* 195—202:—

"Þat þat ilk proper prynce þat paradys weldeȝ, Is displesed at vch a poynt þat plyes to scape. Bot neuer ȝet in no boke brued I herde Þat euer he wrek so wyperly on werk þat he made, Ne venged for no vilté of vice ne synne, Ne so hastyfly watȝ hot for hatel of his wylle, Ne neuer sodenly soȝt vnsoundely to weng, As for *fylpe of þe flesch* þat foles han vsed."

I have quoted the above passages at some length; they show, I think, not only, as was above stated, that the poem of Gaw. is distinctly imbued with religious ideas, but that the descriptive and moral passages as well as the underlying moral of the whole connect it closely with Cleanness. This I consider better accounted for if the Pearl be *not* interposed between them.

Thus much in disproof of the opinion that the Pearl is a transition from Gaw. to the other poems. Moreover there are the following reasons for placing the Pearl the earliest of the four works. It is remarkably isolated. It is rhymed in complicated lyric strophes, in which even the alliteration affords no real point of contact with Gaw. and Cl. and Pat.; since there was alliteration in the poems from which our poet borrowed both his strophe and diction. This diction is nearly akin to that of other allegorical poems; it is without our author's own quaint vigorous phrases. The number of comparisons also is much greater. I have examined the four poems, in this particular, with the following result.

In the 1212 lines of the Pearl there are 25 comparisons (76, 77, 106, 114, 115, 129, 165, 178, 184, 195, 212, 213, 365, 607, 608, 753,

822, 894, 982, 1018, 1026, 1056, 1085, 1112, 1115), and 10 comparisons founded upon the part of the Bible paraphrased (501, 723, 733, 801, 802, 875, 881, 990, 1025, 1106). In all *35* comparisons.

In the first 1212 lines of Gaw. *11* (199, 213, 235, 236, 319, 337, 604, 802, 847, 945, 956). In the remaining 1318 lines 8 (1819, 2102, 2202, 2203, 2293 two comparisons, 2364, 2396).

In the first 1212 lines of Cleanness *17* (222, 223, 226, 554, 556, 790, 791, 886, 966, 984, 1018, 1022, 1035, 1068, 1132, 1134 [1011 suggested by the Bible]. In the remaining 600 lines 7 (1458, 1500, 1581, 1684, 1694, 1696 [1697 suggested by the Bible].

In the 531 lines of Pat. 7 (258, 272, 274, 292, 410, 450, 472), or, taking the proportion, in 1212 lines 15.98 + or *nearly 16* comparisons.

The following is the average result: in the Pearl comparisons occur every 34.62 + lines; in Gaw. every 133.15 + lines; in Cl. every 75.5 lines; in Pat. every 75.85 + lines.

The others poems belong to that sphere of religious thought which deals with human things and with the church militant; the Pearl has its

source in that sunny and transparent sphere which
encircled the Virgin, and in which a more disin-
terested fancy painted to itself the lot of the divi-
nity it worshipped, eternally happy, like the old
gods, the ῥεῖα ζώοντες. The versification of the Pearl
belongs peculiarly to this range of religious conception. Thus No. 24 of the Early Engl. Text Soc.
publications p. 12 is in this same strophe. There
Christ is the "flour and fruyt both softe and sote"
and "full curteis" is his "comeli cus" etc. In the
Pearl ten Brink finds this strophe "eine nach unserm
gefuhl zu dem gegenstand wenig passende form."
It might be juster to call it an unsuitable form for
the manner in which our feeling would conceive the
subject: for thought, language and versification are
in harmony in the poem as it stands: It was doubtless during youth, while his education, like that of
his contemporaries, was completing itself within the
bosom of the church that the poet learned to breathe
in this lyrical and sequestered atmosphere; and the
Pearl as the poem most permeated therewith may
be presumed to fall in the earlier stages of his maturity.

I should therefore place the Pearl the first of
the four poems. We saw reason to believe (cf. p. 18)

that Gaw. preceded Cl., and, as Gaw. and Cl. are so closely connected etc. (cf. p. 33), Pat. would seem to be the last of our poet's works.

_____

The positive date of the four poems.

In this respect little has been done.

Madden rehearses the different views up to the date of his edition (1839): namely, those of Warton, Price,˙ Conybeare, Laing, and Guest. The dates so given range from the 13ᵗʰ century, before Robt. of Brunne, to about 1400. Madden expresses his own opinion, p. 301: — "It will not be difficult from a careful inspection of the manuscript itself, both in regard to the writing and illuminations, to assign it to the reign of Richard the second; and the internal evidence arising from the peculiarities of costume, armour and architecture would lead us to assign the romance to the same period or a little earlier."

Morris sets 1320—1330 upon the title page of his edition of Sir Gawayne. In his and Skeat's

Spec. of E. E. Lit. however he places Cl. and Pat. *before*, and Sir Gaw. *about* 1360.

Trautmann (Über Verf. u. Entst.) refers to Morris' opinion; but selects three passages—Pat. 10, Pat. 31—33, and Cl. 5—16, which as showing the influence of Piers Plowman, lead him to place Cl. and Pat. after its first edition;—*i. e.* not earlier than 1362.

(Considerations relative to the alliterative rhymes induce him to add:— "ich behaupte deswegen auch nicht, dass die All. Poems nach 1362 gedichtet seien; aber ich halte es für wahrscheinlich und würde nicht überrascht sein, wenn sich eines Tages 1370, ja 1380 als das entstehungsjahr derselben herausstellte.")

Ten Brink p. 421 lets our poet appear "in den sechziger oder siebziger jahren des jahrhunderts" and again p. 440:— "Als der Verfasser des Gaw. sein Clannesse und Pacience schrieb, da war das allitterirende Versmass bereits durch eine andere Dichtung *(Piers Plowman)* weit über die Grenze seiner ursprünglichen Heimath hinaus populär geworden." He thus seems to agree with Trautmann although without referring to any influence Piers Plowman may have had upon our author.

I shall try to demonstrate this influence and hope by means of additional passages to make it more than probable that Cl. and Pat. were written after the *2ⁿᵈ edition* of Piers Plowman, that is, after 1377 (cf. Skeat, introd. to his edition of text B. p. 2).

I will mark with a star those passages found in the second edition only.

[In the Pearl and in Gaw. I find no trace of Langland's influence; the expression "wex as wroth as the wind" found in both Gaw. and Pat. as well as in P. Pl. III, 328 was undoubtedly usual at the time; so also the idea of faultlessness in the "five wits" and the frequent reference to them. Cf. Gaw. 640, 2193 and P. Pl. I, 15; XIX 211; XIV, 53.]

The 3 passages in Cl. and Pat. cited by Trautmann are as follows:—

(1.) Pat. 9 :—

"I herde on a halyday at a hyȝe masse."
He must mean to compare this with P. Pl. XIII, 384 of the *2ⁿᵈ edition*:

*"In halydayes at holichirche whan ich herde masse."

(2.) (3.) The personification of Poverty, Pity, Penance etc. in Pat. 31—33, and Cl. 5—16, have a general likeness to many passages in P. Pl.

There are a number of other and more striking resemblances.

In Piers Plowman *XVI 97—126 (I quote according to Skeat, text B) there follows immediately upon the nativity the mention of Christ's "surgerye" and of his healing the sick, blind and crooked; *l.* 113 "he leched lazar" (Lazarus). Christ says thereupon in answer to the accusations of the Jews that he has saved them, healed the blind, and fed the multitude with fishes and five loaves.

In Cl. 1085—1105 the same curious order is followed. The passage is some what too long to quote; I will give it in Morris' marginal version — 1084:— "The child Christ was so clean that ox and ass worshipped him. He hated wickedness and uncleanness and would never touch aught that was vile. Yet there came to him ("as lazares monye") lazars and lepers, lame and blind. Dry and ropsical folk. He healed all with kind speech. His handling was so good that he needed no knife to cut or carve with. The bread he broke more perfectly than could all the tools of Toulouse".

This last detail could never have occurred to our poet *in this connection* had not Piers Pl. in

the same place referred to Math. 14, 9 where
Christ breaks the five loaves.

Exactly the same description, in the same
order, is repeated more succinctly P. Pl. XIX, 120:—

> *"And when he woxen was moore
> In his moder's absence,
> He made lame to lepe,
> And gaf light to blynde,
> And fedde with two fisshes
> And with fyve loves
> Sore a—fyngred folk
> Mo than fyve thousand."

The first six portions of Bible history treated
in Cleanness (cf. Morris' enumeration, preface to his
ed. p. XI ff.) are all found as episodes in Piers
Plowman. Three of these episodes seem to have
left traces in Cl.

The Marriage Feast is used by both poets,
though in a radically different manner, to point the
moral of cleanness. The description of the poultry
in Cleanness seems to me a reminiscence of Piers
Plowman.

P. Pl. XV, 455—57:—

> *"He fedde him with no venysoun no feasauntes y baked,
> But with *foules pat fram hym nolde but folowed his*
> [whistellynge.
> And wyth calves flesshe he fedde pe folke pat he loued."

Cf. Cl. 55 ff.:—

"For my boles & my boreȝ arn bayted & slayne
And my *fedde fouleȝ* fatted with sclaȝt,
My *polyle pat is penne—fed* & partrykes bope."
etc.

The Fall of the Angels P. Pl. I, 109—125 and
especially 115 ff.:—

*"And *mo thowsandes* wip hym pan man coupe noumbre,
Lopen ut wip Lucifer in *lothelich forme*
For thei leueden upon him pat lyed in pis manere
Ponam pedem in aquilone, et similis ero altissimo."

—121:—

"For pryde pat he pult out his peyne hath none ende."

Compare Cl. 205—334 and especially l. 220 ff.:—

"Thikke *powsandeȝ* pro prwen per-oute
Fellen fro the fyrmament, *fendeȝ ful blake.*"

—210:—

"sade pyse wordeȝ:
I schal telde vp my trone in pe tra mountayne
And by lyke to pat lorde pat pe lyft made."

At the end of the description just as in P. Pl.:

"Ne pray hym for no pité, so proud watȝ his wylle."

In the description of the wickedness before the
flood—"Pœnitet me fecisse hominem" is translated by
both authors alike P. Pl. IX, 129:—

"Ðat I maked man now it me athynketh."
(Wright reads for-thynketh.)

Cl. 285:—

"Me forthynke3 ful much pat euer I mon made."

The following passage seems undoubtedly a reminiscence of Piers Plowman. P. Pl. XIV, 39—44:—

*"For lente neuere was lyf but lyfode were shapen
Wher-of or wherefore or where-by to lybbe
Firste pe *wylde worme* vnder weet *erthe*
Fissch to lyue in pe *flode* and in pe fyre pe cryket,
De corlue by kynde of pe eyre moste clennest flesch
[of bryddes,
And *bestes* by grasse and by greyne and by grene rotis."

Cf. 'Cl. 530—537:—

"Vche fowle to pe fly3t pat fypere3 my3t serue,
Vche *fysch* to pe *flod* pat fynne coupe nayte,
Vche *beste* to pe bent pat bytes on erbe3;
Wylde worme3 to her won wrype3 in pe *erpe*
De fox & pe folmarde to pe fryth wynde3,
Herttes to hy3e hepe, hare3 to gorste3,
And lyoune3 & lebarde3 to pe lake ryftes."

In Patience the influence of Piers Plowman is less marked.

Trautmann has noted two instances (1) Pat. 9 and (2) 31—33.

Pat. 1—8, 35—53, and 525—531 in the selection of patience as a theme, and in the emphatic association of patience and poverty the poet moves in the sphere of Piers Plowman. Cf. P. Pl.

XIV *191—192, *214—217, *259, *270—271,
*274. X 342, XI 310. That is to say : though the
poet's poverty among other things had turned his
mind toward the virtue of patience (cf. Pat. 35
"Bot syn I am put to a poynt pat pouerte hatte") ;
yet the thought of insisting in the prologue on their
natural connection was most probably suggested as
above.

The preceding comparison has proved, for Cleanness at least, the influence of Piers Plowman.
1377 is therefore for this poem the *terminus a quo*.
We have before found some reason to assume the
nearer chronological connection of Cl. and Gaw. ;
and the manner of the resemblance — both in the
descriptions of feasts, and all that in Gaw. is more
mystical and less dogmatic — pointed to Gaw. as
the earlier. Besides since Gaw., like the Pearl, betrays no influence of P. Pl., there is therefore no
reason to believe that it was written after 1377.
Assuming that our author read the 2nd ed. of P. Pl.
soon after its appearance and that Cl. was written
while the impression was still fresh, I should place
Gaw. circa 1375—7, and Cl. circa 1378—80.

These dates are sufficiently in accordance with
the opinion of Sir Fred. Madden, and with that of

Trautmann who, though unable to prove a later date than 1362, "would not be surprised" should the poems prove to be written in 1370 and even in 1380.

Patience contains no personal allusion to advancing years; there is therefore no subjective reason for placing it much after the other poems. Nevertheless it has in common with them very few such passages as connect Gaw. and Cl. (Pat. 124:— "Hit may not be pat he is blynde pat bigged vche yȝe." cf. Cl. 583—4:— "Wheper he pat stykked vche a stare in vche steppe yȝe, ȝif hym-self be bore blynde hit is a brod wonder," and Pat. 5—8 cf. Pearl 341—348, quoted p. 8—are slight exceptions); and in regard to Piers Plowman there is none of the vividness of a recent impression. These considerations joined to the stamp of maturity, which ten Brink notes, justify us in counting it as the last of the four poems.

I should therefore place the Pearl before Gawain; Gawain c. 1375—7:— Cleanness 1378—80, and Patience after Cleanness.

II.

COMPARISON OF
SIR GAWAYNE WITH THE ROMAN DE PERCEVAL.

Bibliographic.

Sir Fred. Madden (Syr Gaw. Notes, p. 305 ff.) was the first to discover that the most striking incident in Sir Gawayne was borrowed from Crestien's Perceval. He tells in English the story of Carados and his father the magician, and twice, (twice only) quotes the French words:—namely in his note to Gaw. *l.* 90—99 where he gives the parallel French passage, and again where a few words are cited from the description of the wizard. (These quotations are from the prose romance published in Paris in 1530, which however is a very exact version of Crestien's poem). He does not mention any further correspondence of incident, nor any other verbal analogies, nor reminiscences.

Morley, in his English Writers, refers to Madden and follows him. Morris (ed. Sir Gaw., introd. p. vIII), and ten Brink p. 422 add nothing to Madden's statement; for only to the above mentioned incident can we well apply ten Brink's words:—"Die motive zu demselben *(Sir Gawain)* entlehnte er grossentheils dem „Perceval" des Crestien v. Troies, so jedoch, dass er das, was in der quelle bloss als episode auftritt, *zum kern* seiner darstellung macht." etc.

I believe an exacter comparison to be of some interest for the entire history, in England, of the Arthur romances; insomuch as while lesser poets made exact translations, even this poet is in a manner bound to his author and his book. He is not so at home in the whole domain of the Round Table that, having chosen one incident, the others will come to him at hap-hazard, he scarce knows whence; there suggest themselves to him in preference the figures and episodes of the last book which impressed him; its transitions even are his transitions. We may guess that he could count the manuscripts he had pored over, and still knew the last one best.

I do not mean by this at all to deny the influence of other poems, or the use made of them.

Sir Fred. Madden, in his note to line 1226, thinks that the description of the unlacing of the deer may have been suggested by a similar description in Sir Tristram; in his note to line 1699, he recalls Laȝamon's introduction of the simile of a fox-hunt; in the note to line 2446 he supports the author's conception of Morgne la Faye as an old woman by a passage from the Prophecy of Merlin; line 648, note, he looks upon the Virgin's image on Gawain's shield as imitated from Arthur's shield Pridwen, Geof. of Monmouth IX c. 3. He also (p. 307) finds reason to suppose our author acquainted with the prose romance of Perceval le Gallois, to which I shall refer later.

Ten Brink (p. 422, note) mentions the "thatsache, dass sein gedicht zahlreiche anklänge auch an andere Artusromane enthält."

Sir Gawain is not a translation, not a copy; nor was it a wish of the author to recombine the elements of Perceval, as we make the anagram of a name. He was acquainted with other romances, and used them freely when they presented themselves; but what I believe to be the most remarkable result of the ensuing comparison is the *preponderance* of the Roman de Perceval in his mind during the whole composition of his poem. The strongest influence, side by side with this one, fell to the prose romance of Perceval.

I have already implied that there are many analogous incidents, as well as minor resemblances, which Sir Fr. Madden leaves unnoticed. Following the order of the poem itself, I begin with the less important, and give the details of agreement and disagreement in that part of Sir Gawain, which is confessedly suggested by the story of Carados.

Treatment of the narrative of Carados.

I quote from "Perceval le Gallois, ou le Conte du Graal, publié par Potvin," and make no distinction between Crestien de Troies and his continuators, because it was probably the whole Roman de Perceval that lay before the English poet. (The episode of Carados is not by Crestien.) In what version the poem lay before him is of course uncertain; Potvin rarely cites parallel readings:— when he does, however, it is perhaps the Montpellier manuscript which most accords with the English words.

Arthur speaks (12571 P.):—

> "C'à Pentecouste voel tenir,
> La première qui doit venir,
> Court si grant et si honieste
> C'ains nus hom ne vit si grant feste ;
> Car tant i quic doner del mien
> C'ainc nus n'oï parler de rien
> Que je féisce onques encore,
> Se des dons non que donrai ore
> As barons et as chevaliers."

Cf. Gaw. 37—71.

Common as are such descriptions it yet is probable from the connection that the above French lines suggested the animated English feast; possible, too, that the gifts suggested Christmas gifts; although picturesqueness and the habit of other English romancers might have determined the change of time from Whitsuntide to Christmas. Cf. the Engl. Rom. of Perceval, ed. Halliwell, l. 1803 "Tille the heghe dayes of ȝole were gane."

Kay announces that the meal is served and Arthur answers (P. l. 12628):—

> "Nou ferai, Kex, biaus amis ciers;
> Ne place Dieu que jà m'aviengne
> Que à tel fiest jà court tiegne
> Là j'aie corone portée,
> K'aigue soit prise ne donée
> Devant ce k'estrange novele
> U autre aventure moult bele
> I soit voiant tous avenue;
> La coustume ai ensi tenue
> Toute ma vie jusques chi."

Cf. Gaw. 90—102:—

> "And also anoþer maner meued him eke,
> Þat he purȝ nobelay had nomen, he wolde neuer ete
> Vpon such a dere day, er hym deuised were
> Of sum aventurus þyng an vncoupe tale
> Of sum mayn meruayle, þat he myȝt trawe,

Of alderes, of armes, of oþer auenturus,

....

Þis watȝ þe kynges couñtenaunce where he in court were,
At vch farand fest among his fre meny,
in halle."

For the lines Gaw. 86 and again 89:—

"He watȝ so Joly of his Joyfnes, & sum-quat child gered;"

....

"So bi-sied him his ȝonge blod & his brayn wylde."

Cf. elsewhere in P. 9439 :—

"Qu'il est enfes, le roi Artus."

At this point (Gaw. 107—461) we are con-
fronted by the personage who, together with Gawain,
gives our romance its name, and who at the same
time constitutes a marked divergence from the French
text. It behoves us therefore to examine with care
his conception.

Raynbroune, "the knyȝt of armes grene" is
mentioned in the Carle off Carlile, ed. Madden, *l.* 44.
In the Ballad of the Green Knight, which is founded
upon our romance, the green knight is named Sir
Bredbeddle. In the Ballad of King Arthur and the
King of Cornwall, Sir Bredbeddle, the green knight,
with his "collen brand, Millaine knife and *Danish*
axe" (cf. Gaw. *l.* 2223 "A deneȝ ax nwe dyȝt, þe
dynt with to ȝelde" etc.) appears in the rôle of a

conjurer. Can we from this assume any tradition concerning a green knight, which would have led to his substitution for Elyauros? The last mentioned ballad would seem to imply such a tradition, but, though in other respects wholly different from our Sir Gawain, it may in this one contain a reminiscence. We must therefore, until further notices of the Green Knight are discovered (Compare part III, p. 98) study him as an original creation. As such I believe the green colour may have been suggested as follows.

Vermel and *verd*, in Perceval are the two favorite colours of rich attire: — Cf. also King Alisaunder, ed. Weber I. *l.* 6374 ff:—

> "Fair folk woneth in the este;
> Of al thes lond they lyveth best,
> Clothed in scarlet and grene."

Verd, toward the end of Perceval (cf. *l.* 29823, 31695, 34071) is more frequent; in the old English romances it is almost the rule. Cf. Anturs of Arther, ed. Madden *l.* 353, "Hir gyde was gloryous & gaye, alle of gyrfe (a gresse) grene" (Gaw. *l.* 235: "As growe grene as þe gres"); also Perceval of Galles (ed. Halliwell) lines 265 and 277; and Sir Degrevant (ed Halliwell) l. 1604. Moreover the prominence of "li Chevaliers Vermaus" in Perceval might suggest a green counterpart.

As such I believe him to be traceable as follows. In both poems the knight enters, as it were in response to Arthur's demand for adventure; nevertheless he does not come to fight. *The green knight* emphasizes his *peaceful* coming both by word and symbol.

Gaw. *l.* 279: —

"Nay frayst I no fyʒt, in fayth I þe telle."

l. 265: —

"Ʒe may be seker bi þis braunch þat I bere here
Þat I passe as in pes, & no plyʒt seche."

This branch is a "holyn bobbe", *l.* 207:

"Þat is grattest in grene when ʒreues ar bare."

The following quotations will show the association, within this class of romances, between green attire and the bearing, primarily of an olive branch, in sign of peace.

Geof. of Monm. liber. IX c. 15, 11: — "ecce duodecim viri maturæ ætatis, reverendi vultus, ramos olivæ, in signum legationis in dextris ferentes."

King Alisaunder *l.* 1702: —

"And eche with a braunche of olyve
That was tokenyng of pes & lyve."

Ellis Spec. E. E. Metr. Rom., ed. 1805, I, p. 356 : —

"The maiden is ready for to ride,
In a full rich aparaylment,
Of samyte green, with mickle pride
....
A dwarf shall wende by her side;
....
Such were the manners in that tide,
When a maid on a message went."

Ellis p. 360. After peace is made and Lancelot
and his knights lead back the queen to Arthur,

"The other knights, everichone,
In *samyte green* of heathen land,
And their kirtles, ride alone;
And each knight a green garland;
Saddles set with riche stone;
Each one a *branche of olive* in hand."

P. 363 a maid is sent on an embassy : —

"Her 'parayl all of one hue,
Of a *green* velvèt;
In her hand a *branch new*,
For why that no man should her let."

Gaw. *l.* 175:

"A green hors gret and pikke."

In regard to this green colour of his horse and
of all appurtenances, cf. Ipomydon (ed. Weber II)
l. 643 ff. : —

"He purueyd hym iij noble stedes
And also thre noble wedys : —

That one was white as any mylke
The trappure of him was white sylke,
That other was rede, bothe styffe & stoure
The trappure was of the same couloure,
Blake than was that other stede
The same colour was his wede."

To each steed belongs a greyhound of the same colour. Thus our author, having once arrived at green for the attire of the knight, would naturally give him a green steed.

In Perceval of Galles, founded upon the French Perceval, "li chevaliers vermaus" reappears *l.* 605 as the Red knight with "blode red wede, prekande one a rede stede" and again with "blode red stede". It may be observed that the mother of this Red Knight is a witch, as is, in the Ballad of the Green Knight, the Green Knight's mother-in-law.

Green is undoubtedly a more unnatural colour even than blood-red; and is moreover extended to the knight's own person:—but it is a' fairy colur and apt for wonders:—found also as the hue of hair in many kinds of myths and legends and in no wise as amazing as would have been, for instance, blue or purple.

I now resume the description of the feast before the appearance of the Green Knight.

P. *l.* 12638 :—

> "À çou qu'il *parloient* ensi
> Et li autre fisent em pais,
> Parmi l'entrée dou palais
> Voient entrer un chevalier
> *Moult grant,* sour ·ɪ· fauve destrier."

Cf. Gaw. 107 :—

> "Thus per stondes in stale pe stif kyng his-seluen
> *Talkkande* bifore pe hyʒe table" etc. —

l. 136 :—

> "Þer hales in at pe halle dor an agþlich mayster,
> *On pe most on pe molde on mesure hyghe.*"

P. *l.* 12643 :—

> "Viestu d'un peliçon hermine
> Qui jusqu'à tière li traïne;
> En son cief ot .ɪ. capelet,
> A .ɪ. ciercle d'or de bounet."

Cf. Gaw. 153 :—

> "A mere mantile abof, mensked with-inne,
> With pelure pured apert pe pane ful clene."

P. *l.* 12647 :—

> "S'ot çainte une *moult longue* espée
> Qui de *fin or* fu enheudée
> Et les *renges d'un cier orfroi.*"

Cf. Gaw. 208 :—

> "And an ax in his oper, *a hoge* and *vn-mete*".

—210:—

"Þe hede of an elnȝerde þe large lenkþe hade,
Þe grayn al of grene stele and *of golde* hewen."

—217:—

"A *lace lapped aboute*, þat louked at þe hede,
And so after þe halme halched ful ofte,
Wyth tryed tasseleȝ perto tacched in-noghee."

Per. *l.* 12650:—

"Tout à ceval vint jusqu'al dois
Et dist en haut mouet gentement:
Rois Artu." etc.

Cf. Gaw. 221 ff:—

"Þis haþel heldeȝ hym in, & þe halle entres,
Driuande to þe heȝe dece, dut he no woþe,
Haylsed he neuer one, bot heȝe he ouer loked.
Þe fyrst word þat he warp, 'wher is'; he sayd,
'Þe gouernour of þis gyng?" etc.

P. *l.* 12655:—

"Rois, fait-il, ·i· don vos demanc."

—12658—12670:—

"Vous le saurés
Colée demanc, sans deçoivre,
Por un autre errant à reçoivre.'
'Chevalier, que me dites-vous?'
'Rois, je vos di tout à estrous
Que, s'il a çaiens chevalier
Qui la tieste me puist trencier
A .i. seul cop de ceste espée,

Et se repuis de le colée
Apriès saner et regarir,
Séurs puet estre, sans falir,
D'ui en .i. an d'ausi reprendre
La colée, s'il l'ose atendre."

Cf. Gaw. 272 ff. : —

"Bot if þou be so bold as alle burneȝ tellen,
Þou wyl grant me godly þe gomen þat I ask,
bi ryȝt."

—285 : —

"If any so hardy in þis hous holdeȝ hym-seluen,
Be so bolde in his blod, brayn in hys hede,
Þat dar stifly strike a strok for an oþer."

—294 : —

"And I schal stonde hym a strok, stif on þis flet
Elleȝ þou wyl diȝt me þe dom to dele hym an oþer,
barlay ;
And ȝet gif hym respite,
A twelmonyth and a day ;
Now hyȝe, and let se tite
Dar any her-inne oȝt say."

P. l. 12673 : —

"Mais n'i a nul qui l'ost ballier."

—12678 : —

"Ha ; fait li chevaliers, 'signor,
Et çou qui est? n'en ferés plus ?
Or puet véoir li rois Artus
Que sa cours n'est mie si rice
Comme cascuns dist et afice ;

N'i a nul chevalier hardi;
Por voir le vos tesmogne ci
Que jou dirai teles novièles
Qui n'ièrent ne plaisant ne beles."

Cf. Gaw. 301:—

"If he hem stowned vpon fyrst, stiller were panne
Alle pe hered-men in halle, pe hyȝ & pe loȝe."

—309:—

"What, is pis arpures hous', quod pe hapel penne,
'Þat al pe rous rennes of, purȝ ryalmes so mony?
Where is now your sourquydrye & your conquestes,
Your gryndel-layk, & your greme, & your gretè wordes?
Now is pe reuel & pe renoun of pe rounde table
Ouer-walt wyth a worde of on wyȝes speche;
For al dares for drede, with-oute dynt schewed."

Per. l. 12687:—

"Aler s'en voloit aïtant,
Quant Caradeus sali avant,
Qui noviaus chevaliers estoit."

Arthur discourages Carados:— 12698:—

"Çaiens a maint bon chevalier,
Qui ausi bien et mius ferroient
Que vous, se faire le voloient."

When Carados presents himself the following
lines occur in the Montpellier Manuscript:—

"Estes-vous au meillor eslir?"
Certes, nennil, mès au plus fol."

Cf. Gaw. 354:—

"I am þe wakkest, I wot, and of wyt feblest,
And lest lur of my lyf, quo laytes þe sope,
Bot for as much as ȝe ar myn em, I am only to prayse
No bounté bot your blod I in my bodé knowe."

The great humility here attributed to Gawain
may be a reminiscence of Arthur's other nephew,
Carados, the untried knight. Precisely as Carados'
adventure is here transferred to Gawain, so also are
transferred to him, in Crestien, various adventures
which Rob. de Borron ascribes to Perceval in his
"Perceval ou la Quête du St-Graal" (publié Huchier
1865).

Per. *l.* 12706:—

"Devers le dois cil se retorne,
Le cief baissié, le col estent;
Caradeus fiert si durement
Que la tieste voler en fist.
Desor le dois cil reprist
Par les keviaus, à ses .II. mains,
Ausi com s'il fust trestous sains."

Cf. Gaw. 417:—

"The grene knyȝt vpon grounde graypely hym dresses,
A littel lut with þe hede, þe leré he discouereȝ,
His longe louelych lokkeȝ he layd ouer his croun,
Let þe naked nec to þe note schewe.
Gauan gripped to his ax, & gederes hit on hyȝt."

—427:—

"Þe fayre hede fro þe halce hit felle to þe erþe,
Þat fele hit foyned wyth her fete, þere hit forth roled."

Gaw. *l.* 433:

"Laȝt to his lufly hed, & lyft hit vp sone."

In both poems the head speaks after it has
been cut off:—

Perc. *l.* 12719:—

"Caradieu', fait li chevaliers,
'D'ui en ·I· an biaus amis ciers,
Reserai chi, ce saciés bien;
Si ne laissiés por nul rien
Que je ne vos truisse à cele eure."

Cf. Gaw. 448:—

"Loke, Gawan, þou be graype to go as þou hetteȝ."

—455:—

"For-þi me for to fynde if þou fraysteȝ, faylez þou neuer,
Þer-fore com, oþer recreaunt be calde þe be-houeus."

Perc. *l.* 12724:—

"Atant s'en va, plus ne demeure;
Et li rois tous pensius remaint;
Avœc lui ot chevalier maint
Qui sont dolant et esmari."

Cf. Gaw. *l.* 457:—

"With a runisch rout þe rayneȝ he torneȝ,
Halled out at þe hal-dor, his hed in his hande."

....

4

—*l.* 467:—

"Þaȝ Arþer þe hende kyng at hert hade wonder,
He let no semblaunt be sene etc."

The English lines seem an intentional correction of the French.

The return of the enchanter at the close of the year (Perc. 12745 — 12840) has little in common with the second meeting of Gawain and the Green Knight.

But in the prose romance quoted by Madden as Hélie de Boron's Roman du Graal, and published, as 1ère partie, in Potvin's edition of Perceval li Gallois, this adventure of Carados is attributed to Lancelot. The prose romance, according to Dr. Birch-Hirschfeld, ("Die Sage v. Gral", p. 142) was written in the second quarter of the thirteenth century. Sir. Fr. Madden suggests as probable that our poet knew both versions and combined them. A comparison made by me before I could obtain Madden's Gawayne renders the acquaintance with the prose Perceval almost certain.

Compare, p. 103 of the prose romance, the description of the knight who is to be beheaded by Lancelot. He appears in a jewelled dress and

"estoit vestuz d'une coste vermeille courte, ...
et tenoit *une grant hache.*"

Gaw. *l.* 152 :—

"A strayt cote ful stre3t, pat stek on his sides."

....

—*l.* 208 :—

"And an ax in his oper, a hoge and vn-mete."

Perc. p. 104 :—

The knight requires Lancelot to swea· ·on the
relics that he will return in a year.

Cf. Gaw. where an oath is expressly waived.

l. 403 :—

"And pat I swere þe for sope, and by my seker traweþ'.
'Þat is in-nogh in nwe 3er, hit nedes no more."

Perc. p. 233 :—

Lancelot returns in a year's time to receive
the blow, "se dresce, si se met à jenoillons et
estant le col. Li chivaliers entoise la hache;
Lanceloz ot venir le cop, si beisse le chief et la
hache passe outre. Il li dist: 'sire chevaliers,
ainsint ne fist mie mes frères que vos océistes, ainz
tint le chief et le col tout quoi et ausint vos cou-
vient-il feire."

Compare Gaw. *l.* 2265 :—

"Bot Gawayn on þat giserne glyfte hym bysyde,
As hit com glydande adoun, on glode hym to schende,
And schranke a lytel with þe schulderes, for þe scharp yrne."

— *l.* 2270 :—

"Þou art not Gawayn,' quod þe gome, 'þat is so goud halden."

— *l.* 2274 :—

"Nawþer fiked I, ne flaȝe, freke, quen þou myntest,
Ne kest no kauelacion, in kyngeȝ hous Arthor,
My hede flaȝ to my fote, & ȝet flaȝ I neuer."

Perc. p. 233 :—

Two damoiseles interpose and the knight asks forgiveness of Lancelot, "comme au plus loial chevalier del monde."

Compare Gaw. where the Green Knight calls Gawain "þe fautlest freke, þat euer on fote ȝede."

The substitution indeed of an axe for a sword and of a short coat for a flowing mantel (or rather in Gaw. both short coat and mantle are retained), together with the reference to an oath, would not be enough in itself to prove any knowledge of the prose romance; but that Gawain also flinches from the blow, and is reproved in like fashion is not a trait to be twice invented.

Gawain and Guigambresil.

If the adventure of Carados is the actual theme of our story, yet there is another adventure which, though subordinated, halves with it the poem; which fills the interstices, and gives solidity to the frame work; and of which we may say that, when the English poet conceived his work, it was present to him simultaneously with that of Carados, and not remembered as an accessory. This second adventure, attributed by Crestien himself to Gawain, is so finely adapted to its end, so modified and redistributed, that its original form has hitherto been overlooked. It is to be found in that part of Crestien which may be called the adventure with Guigambresil.

At the time when the "Damoisele hydeuse" has damped the joy of Perceval's return, there appears before the court (P. *l.* 6129) Guigambresil, who lays his lord's murder to Gawain's charge. Upon this insult Gawain challenges Guigambresil and wanders forth in search of him. Cf. the general grief with that at Gawain's departure in our poem.

Perc. *l.* 6184 ff:—

> "Ains que il fust de cort méus,
> Ot apriés lui moult grant duel fet,
> Maint pis batu, maint ceviel tret."

....

—*l.* 6190:—

"Grant duel en font maintes et maint."

Gaw. *l.* 558:—

"Þere watȝ much derne doel driuen in þe sale
Þat so worthe as Wawan schulde wende on þat ernde."

....

—*l.* 672:—

"Al þat seȝ þat semly syked in hert."

....

—*l.* 684:—

"Wel much watȝ þe warme water þat waltered of yȝen."

In the scene at court between Gawain and Guigambresil, there is but one other knight mentioned
by name: Agrevain li orguilleus, Gawain's brother,
who begs him to refute the accusation. It may be
on account of this association that he is among the very
few named at the banquet which the green knight
breaks in upon.—Gaw. *l.* 110:—"Agrauayn a la dure
mayn." This epithet which Madden, notes p. 110,
criticizes as "never applied to him in the romances"
occurs, nevertheless, *l.* 9510 of Perceval. Cf. 9509 ff.:—

"Et li secons est Agrevains,
Li *orguilleus as dures mains.*"

And we cannot but find in this adaptation
of an ἅπαξ λεγόμενον an evidence of minute acquaintance with the French poem.

After many adventures Gawain meets a hunt Perc. *l.* 7085 ff. One of the knights greets Gawain and tells him to go to his castle where he will find his sister. He sends a message to her, concerning Gawain.

Perc. *l.* 7115:—

"Et k'ele autant face de lui
Com de moi ki ses frères sui;
Tel *solas et tel compagnie*
Li face qu'il ne li griet mie
Quant nos seromes revenue."

Compare Gaw. (1096—1100) the speech of the Green Knight, when he asks Gawain to remain in the castle during the hunt.

Gaw. *l.* 1097:—

"And to mete wende,
When ȝe wyl, wyth my wyf, þat wyth you schal sitte,
And *comfort yow with compayny*, til *I to cort torne*,
ȝe lende."

The lady receives the message.

Perc. *l.* 7183:—

"Et cele dist, ki grant joie a:
'Benéois soit ki m'en voia
Tel companie come ceste."

l. 7213 an attendant enters:—

"Si les trova entre-baisant
Et moult très grant joie faisant."

He arouses the household against whom Gawain
defends himself until the knights, who prove to be
the king and Guigambresil, return from the hunt:—
and the duel between Gawain and Guigambresil is
deferred a year. Compare Gaw. l. 2374—2394 with
the following lines spoken by Gawain.

Perc. l. 7553:—

> "N'ai pas de ma mort tel paor
> Que jà mius ne voelle à honor
> La mort soffrir et endurer
> Que vivre à honte et parjurer'.
> 'Biaus sire, fait li vavasours
> Il ne vous est jà deshonours."

In both accounts therefore does Gawain leave
Arthur's court on an enterprise of life and death.
The description of the grief at his departure is common
to both. In both he wanders forth in search of his
adversary and encounters many adventures.

Cf. Gaw. l. 715:—

> "At vche warpe oper water per pe wyȝe passed,
> He fonde a foo hym byfore, bot ferly hit were,
> And pat so foule & so felle, pat feȝt hym by-hode;
> So mony meruayl bi mount per pe mon fyndeȝ,
> Hit were to tore for to telle of pe tenpe dole."

In Crestien he meets his unknown enemy who
directs him to his castle, just as in Gaw. he comes
to the castle of the Green Knight without know-

ing who his host is. In Perceval the lord of
the castle sends Gawain to be entertained by his
sister while he is out hunting, just as in the English
romance Gawain is left with the wife of the Green
Knight during the three hunts. The same instructions
are given to wife and sister respectively, "to comfort him with company" till the hunt is over. In
both romances Gawain is received with open arms;
and he and the lady kiss and make great merriment.
Our poet does indeed rescue Gawain's chastity; but
preserves the colouring of the original in so much
as Gawain, by the acceptance of the green lace,
becomes guilty of a breach of faith. In both romances,
again, Gawain's treachery is discovered by his unknown host:—this host is in the one case, the
Green Knight, whom he sought; in the other, the
son of the lord whose murder is laid to Gawain's
charge:—in his castle, as his retainer and companion,
is that Guigambresil whom Gawain seeks. In Perceval the impending duel is then deferred for a year;
in the English romance Gawain escapes with a slight
blow. In both Gawain is assured that his honour
is safe.

It results from this summary that we may
regard our English poem in two ways. We can

look upon it as the adventure of Carados with the insertion of Gawain's adventure with Guigambresil; or as the adventure with Guigambresil modified by the effective substitution, for the duel, of the episode of Carados. What decides in favour of the former, is the poet's own handling of the two; he himself with the imaginative, half mystic treatment, which is the part of his work most truly his own, lays the stress upon the adventure of Carados.

Crestien's influence in the elaboration.

There remain to be considered such modifications of given scenes as may have been suggested by other portions of the French Perceval, not originally connected with the subject matter of our poem.

Gawain's temptations in the castle of the Green Knight seem to me to contain a reminiscence of three other of his adventures, two of which are found in Crestien, and one in the prose Perceval.

Perc. l. 32173 ff. a lady speaks:—

> "Sire, se Damledex m'aït,
> Et si me doinst joie et santé,
> Onques home de mère né
> N'aimai par amors se vos non;
> Car vous iestes de tel renom
> Que je vous ai amé piéça,

Si tieng que mon damage i a
Isi que vous ne m'amés mie
Car *vous avés plus bele amie,*
Au mien quidier, que jou ne soi."

Compare Gaw. 1268—1275 : —

"Bi Mary,' quod þe menskful, 'me pynk hit anoþer,
For were I worth al þe wone of wymmen alyue,
And al þe wele of þe worlde were in my honde,
And I schulde chepen & chose, to cheue me a lorde,
For þe costes þat I haf knówen vpon þe knyȝt here,
Of bewté & debonerté, & blype semblaunt,
And þat I haf er herkkened, & halde hit here trwee,
Þer schulde no freke vpon folde bifore yow be chosen.*"

— *l.* 1782 : —

"*Bot if ȝe haf a lemman, a leuer, þat yow lykeȝ better,*" etc.

Gawain tells his name to a *pucele* whom
he has rescued and she replies : —

Perc. *l.* 37898 ff. : --

"Sire dist elle, querredon
Vous doi, *tout vous mec à bandon*
Mon cors, et trestot mon avoir,
Car je ne doi nul gré savoir
Fors à vous, sans plus, de ma vie."

Cf. Gaw. 1237 ff. : —

"Ȝe ar welcum to my cors,
Yowre awen won to wale,
Me be-houeȝ of fyne force,
Your seruaunt be and schale."

And again the same *pucele.*

Percev. *l.* 38484 :—

> "Lors a *Gauvain en ses bras pris,*
> *Si l'estraint suëf et embrace,*
> Les iols li baise et puis la face."

Gaw. answers, Perc. *l.* 38514 :—

> "Bièle,' fait-il, 'se Dex me voie,
> Ne puet estre, aler me couvient,
> Que jou ai à faire à Carduel."

Compare Gaw. *l.* 1305 at the conclusion of the same interview :—

> "Ho comes nerre with pat, & *cacheȝ hym in armeȝ,*
> *Louteȝ luflych adoun, & pe leude kysseȝ.*"

In the prose Perceval with which we have already seen that our author was acquainted, page 67—68 :—

> "Et quant il (Gawain) fu couchier, cles s'assiéent devant lui et ont le cierge alumé, et s'apuient sor la couche et li presantent mout lor service. Mesire Gauvains ne lor respont autre chose que: 'granz merciz'; car il panssa à dormir et à reposer. 'Par Dieu' fet l'une à l'autre, 'se ce fust Monseignor Gauvains, li niés le roi Artu, il parlast à nos autrement, et trouveissions en lui plus de déduit que en cestui. Mes cist est uns Gauvains contrefez: malement est emploiee l'anor que l'an li a feite."

Cf. Gaw. *l.* 1293 :—

> "Bot pat ȝe be Gawan, hit gotȝ in mynde."

—1297:—

"So god as Gawayn gaynly is halden,
And cortaysye is closed so clene in hym-seluen
Couth not lyʒtly haf lenged so long wyth a lady,
Bot he had craued a cosse, bi his courtaysye."

—1481:—

"Sir, ʒif ʒe be Wawan wonder me pynkkeʒ."

Again; in Crestien (*l*. 10102) when Gawain comes to the *enchanted* castle he finds two queens there:—an older, Arthur's mother Ugierne, and a younger, his own mother (10102). In our poem where the two ladies appear in the same way, the older leading the younger (*l*. 947, cf. P. 9475) the older proves to be "Morgne the faye" Arthur's half sister, Gawain's aunt. Both of these relationships are particularly mentioned. Is it not probable, in view of our poets habit of receiving suggestions from Perceval, that that other adventure had a share in this one?

Madden in his note to *l*. 2446 quotes a few sentences from the Prophecies of Merlin to show that Morgan la Fay was not always conceived as young; but the passage proves also that she retained a semblance of youth. Madden seems to me to begin wrongly in supposing the form in which

Gawain saw Morgain to have been her own. Our poet probably imagined, what is often found, an older lady as the companion of the young châtelaine. As above mentioned, a remembrance of the two ladies in the enchanted castle probably suggested to him, in the elder, a relative of Gawain; and Morgain, Arthur's relative also, the great enchantress, was an appropriate immate of the Green Knight's castle. The atmosphere of sorcery which so changed the Green Knight as to make him unrecognizable affected Morgain as well, whom our poet represents as the author of the whole adventure. This gave him the opportunity to introduce that description of diabolical hideousness in which romance writers have delighted since first Crestien took from Robert de Borron "la damoisele hydeuse." While our author has applied this description to Morgain *la Fay*, Gautier de Doulens, one of Crestien's continuators, closes the same description with the words (Perc. *l.* 25744):—

"Je ne sai s'ele fu *faée*."

In other old english romances I have found but one similar description and that (in the Weddynge of Sir Gaw. and Dame Ragnell, and in the Marriage of Sir Gaw.) is, as I shall show later, most probably from the same source.

I give a portion of Crestien's description, and the greater part of that in Gaw.:—although the latter is distinguished both by the omission of the most loathsome comparisons and by new traits peculiar to old age.

Perc. *l.* 5998:—

"Ains ne véistes *si noir fer*
Come ele ot *les mains* et *le cors;*
Mais del mains estoit çou encor,
À l'autre laidesse qu'ele ot;
Quant si *oel* èrent andui clot,
Petit èrent con oel de rat;
Ses *nés* fu de singe u de cat,
Et ses *lèvres* d'asne u de buef;

....

—6011:—

Et s'ot *les rains et les epaules,*
Trop bien faites por metre baules;
S'ot bas le dos et hances tortes,
Qui vont ausi com ·II· rootes,
Bien sont fait por mener dance."

Cf. Gaw. 957:—

"Þat oper wyth a gorger watȝ gered ouer þe swyre,
Chymbled ouer hir *blake chyn* with mylk-quyte vayles,

....

—*l.* 961:—

Þat noȝt watȝ bare of þat burde bot þe *blake broȝes,*
Þe tweyne *yȝen* & þe *nase,* þe *naked lyppeȝ,*
And þose were soure to se & sellyly blered;
A mensk lady on molde mon may hir calle,
                for gode;

Hir body watȝ schort & pik,
Hir buttokeȝ bay and brode,
More lykker-wys on to lyk,
Watȝ pat scho hade on lode."

The chapel at which Gàwain meets the Green Knight and of which he says *l.* 2191 :—

"Wel bisemeȝ pe wyȝe wruxled in grene
Dele here his deuocioun, on pe deueleȝ wyse."

reminds one faintly of the "chapelle perilleuse" in the prose Perceval.

The name of Gawain's horse *Gryngolet,* of which Madden (note to *l.* 597) says that it is "an additional proof of our author's knowledge of *French romances,*" proves only his knowledge of *Perceval,* where *Gringolet* is mentioned at least seven times (*l.* 7583, 8498, 11101, 11924, 31542, 31410, 32926 ff.).

The order of reception and entertainment upon Gawain's arrival at the castle of the Green Knight (*l.* 816—887) recalls Perceval's arrival at the castle of the Fisher King (Perc. *l.* 4247—4458) but The Anturs of Arther, stanza xxv, and Sir Isumbras, stanza LXXXVII, show that at least the latter part of the description had become stereotyped.

The arming of Gawain (*l.* 567—622) resembles, at least by its unusual length of detail and by the laying down of the carpet, the lines 19014 ff. of Perceval where Gawain is armed by Arthur and the court:—the description of a strange castle (as in lines 764—803 of Gaw.) occurs frequently throughout the French romances, but is nowhere so frequent as in Perceval (*l.* 2513 ff., 4228 ff., 8025 ff., 8592 ff., to mention those by Crestien only); and in no other poem could our author have found *as much* suggestion of wild and distant ways traversed in search of a great trial; of tests and of forebodings; or, as we see from the direction which the poetry of the Grail has uniformly taken, of guilt and repentance, and of a spiritualized knighthood.

I have noticed the following points of contact with other English romances.

The Anturs of Arther (I quote according to Madden's ed.), written before Sir Gaw. and the Gr. Kn. (cf. ten Brink, p. 420), and probably suggesting its metrical form, contains a description of a hunt very similar to that in Sir Gaw. Cf. lines 1136—1177, and 1319—1324 with the 28 lines in the Anturs of Art., and especially:—

"To felle of þe *femmales* in þe foreste wele frythede
Faire in the *fernysone tyme*, by frythis and fellis."

5

Cf. Gaw. 1156 :—

"For þe fre lorde hade de-fende in *fermysoun tyme,*
Þat þer schulde *no mon meue to þe male dere.*"

Anturs :—

"Under þose bewes þay bade, þose baryns so bolde,
To *bekire at þose barrayne, in bankis so bare.*"

Cf. Gaw. 1319:—

"And ay þe lorde of þe lond is lent on his gamneȝ,
To *hunt in holteȝ and hepe at hyndeȝ barayne.*"

Anturs :—

" *Thay keste of* paire *copilles* in clyffes so calde."

Cf. G. 1147 :—

" *Couples* huntes *of kest.*"

Anturs :—

"Herkyn *huntynge* with *hor̄es* in holtis so hare."

Cf. G. 1165 :—

" *Huntereȝ* wyth hyȝe *horne* hasted hem after."

Anturs :

"And by þe *stremys* so *strange* þat swyftly swoghes
Þay *wery* þe wilde swyne & wyrkkis þame waa."

Cf. G. 1169 :—

"Bi þay were tened at þe hyȝe, & *taysed to þe wattreȝ.*"

Anturs :—

" *Grete hundis* in the greues *fulle gladly gā̄e gaa.*"

Cf. G. 1171 :—·

"& þe *gre-houndeȝ so grete, þat geten hem bylyue.*"

King Horn (ed. Mætzner) *l.* 565 ff. Rymenhild gives
  Horn a magic ring.

Sir Eglamour of Artois (ed. Halliwell "Thornton
  Romances"). Organata gives Eglamour a ring
  with the words, 620:—

> "And that rynge be upon youre honde
> Ther schalle nothyng yow slon."

Sir Perceval of Galles (ed. Halliwell):—

l. 1859 ff.:—

> "In alle this werlde wote I nane
> Siche stone in a rynge:
> A mane that hat it in were,
> One his body for to bere,
> There scholde no dyntys hym dere,
> Ne to the dethe brynge."

Cf. Gaw. 1852:—

> "While he hit (the green lace) hade hemely halched aboute,
> Þer is no hapel vnder heuen to-hewe hym þat myȝt."

It is interesting to notice that the wife of
the Gr. Kn. first offers Gaw. a gold ring (cf.
l. 1817) which probably had the same magical
qualities as the lace.

S. Gaw. and the Carle of Carelyle.

This romance has a number of resemblances.
(Cf. especially the temptation of Gaw.)

Kyng Alisaunder (ed. Weber):—

l. 7709 ff.:—

> "Adam was byswike of Eve;
> And Sampson theo fort, also.
> Daliada dude him wrong and wo;
> And Davyd the kyng was brougbt of lyf,
> Thorugh the gyle of his wyf;
> And Salamon, for a woman's love,
> Forsok his God that syt above."

Sir Gaw. consoles himself by the enumeration of the same personages.

l. 2416:—

> "For so watʒ Adam in erde with one bygyled,
> & Salamon with fele sere, & Samson eft soneʒ,
> Dalyda dalt hym hys wyrde, & Dauyth per-after
> Watʒ blended with Barsabe, þat much bale poled."

III.

SIR GAWAIN IN ENGLISH POEMS.

Sir Fred. Madden (in the introd. to "Syr Gaw. a collect. of rom. poems etc.") treats exhaustively the Gawain-saga from Geoffrey of Monmouth to its latest development in the French prose romances, touching also upon the Welsh, the English, the Low and Old High German translation-literature.

There could not be English Hartmanns, Wolf-
rams and Gottfrieds to translate, or elaborate in
their entirety the Arthur-romances; at the time
when these had most interest the French originals
were read, and French was written at the English
court. What exists in the language of the people
is also more popular in character; it betrays ignorance
of courtly customs; it represents the taste and choice
of the *English* public to whom these stories filtered
down, and therefore it seems interesting to do what
Madden has not done:—*i. e.* to note the attitude
toward Gawain of the English poems, as such, in
all cases where they differ from their immediate
original. It is not that we have to expect from them
many new incidents, or any standpoint not found in
some French poem:—their choice of incident is, in
most cases, their verdict. To Gawain this choice is
supremely favourable; from Laȝamon on we shall
find him the popular English hero, on him is heaped
every epithet of praise and stories in his honour are
retold more gladly than those celebrating the other
knights of the Round Table.

The Arthurian romances may be divided into
two classes:—I, those founded upon Geof. of Monmouth and describing Arthur's birth, conquests and

death, and II, those treating adventures supposed to occur during the twelve years of peace mentioned by Geof.

I. THE ROMANCES BASED UPON GEOF. OF MONMOUTH.

1. *Laȝamon's translation of Wace.*

This is the first treatment of the Arthurian tradition in the English language. Living in the West of England at the beginning of the 13th cent., Laȝ. is supposed to have drawn in part upon native tradition in the many additions he made to the chronicle of Wace. Prof. Wülcker (Paul & Braune, Beiträge III, p. 555) was the first to call attention to the greater rôle played by Gawain. He has instanced three examples:—Laȝ. III, 61 ff., cf. Wace II, 175; Laȝ. III, 132 ff., cf. Wace II, 223, and the Engl. and French accounts of Gawain's death.

A careful comparison of Wace and Laȝamon yields the following results.

Wace (ed. Leroux de Lincy) II, p. 30 mentions Anna's marriage to Lot:—

> "De li fut nés li quens Walwains
> Qui tant fu preudom de ses mains."

In the parallel passage Laȝ. (ed. Madden) II, 385 ff. there is no mention of Gaw. This is the

only instance (cf. p. 74 and p. 75 later which are
only formal exceptions) I have found where Gawain
is mentioned by Wace and not by Laʒ. The relation is always reversed.

Wace II, 69, cf. Laʒ. II, 509. Wace mentions
Gaw. as a little child. Laʒ., in addition, makes
Arthur say of Gaw. and Modred.

"Þeo me beoð ō londe children alre leofest."

Laʒ. II, 546 :—

"Suð inne Cornwali per Walwain wes for faren.
And him seolf (Arthur) wes for-wuded."

is not in Wace and shows that an inaccurate tradition had joined Gawain's death to that of Arthur.
—Wace II, 79 in praise of Gaw.:—

"Prous fu et de mult grant mesure,
D'orgoil et de forfait n'ot gure ;
Plus vaut faire que il ne dist
Et plus doner qu'il ne pramist."

Cf. Laʒ. II, 554 ff. :—

"Wælle wel wes hit bitoʒen pat Walwai wes to monne
[iboren."

Laʒ. in his translation, gives a more abstract
and "model" colouring and thus strikes the tone in
regard to Gawain, which we shall find in the later
English romances.

Laȝ. II, 577 as the British army marches out
to the duel between Frolle and Arthur:—

"þeo (fifti hundred) Wælwain lædde, þe wæs a wæl-kempe."

Laȝ. II, 585 after the combat Arthur calls:

"Whær ært þu Walwain monne me leofest."

Neither of these passages is in Wace.

Wace II, 121—122 Gawain answers Cador's speech:—

> "Sire quens, dist Gauwains, par foi,
> Por noiant estes en esfroi:
> Bone est la pais après la guerre,
> Plus rice et mildre en est li terre.
> Mult sunt bones les gaberies,
> Si deduit et les drueries;
> Por la noblesce de sa amie
> Fait jouenes hom cevalerie."

Cf. Laȝ. II, 626—627:—

"Þat iherde Walwain, þe wes Ardures mæi,
And wraddede hine wid Cador swide þe pas wond kende,
And þus answærede Walwain þe sele,
'Cador þu ært a riche mon, þine ræddes ne beoð noht idon.
For god is grið & god is frið, þe freoliche þer haldeð wið,
And godd sulf hit makede þurh his godd-cunde,
For grið makeð godne mon gode workes wurchen.
For alle monnen bið þa bet, þat lond bið þa murgre."

We see here a very different nuance; Gawain,
instead of desiring peace that the young knights
may practise lovemaking and chivalry, looks upon

it as a time for good works. This <u>tendency to</u>
make Gawain the <u>mouth piece</u> of sententious <u>moral</u>
<u>remarks</u> will be found later, and is not to be
wholly attributed to the fact that <u>La3amon</u> was a
priest.

Wace II, 138 Arthur intrusts his kingdom to
Modred, "chevalier prou et mervillos".

La3. III, 9 adds:

"He wes Walwainnes broðer, næs per nan oðer."

and p. 10:—

"Ah men to soðe i-wenden for Walwain wes his broðer.
Þe alre treowest pe tuhte to pan hirede;
Þurh Walwain wes Modræd monnē pa leouere.
And Arður pe kene ful wel him iquemde."

Wace II, 162:—

> "A ses deus a Gauvain josté
> Qui à Rome ot lonc tans esté,
> Por ce qu'il erent bien prisié,
> Bien honoré, et ensagnié."

Cf. La3. III, 43:—

"Þe 3et pe king cleopede Walwæin pe wes his deoreste mæi
For Walwain cuðe Romanisc, Walwain cuðe Bruttisc.
He wes iued in Rome wel feole wintre."

Madden (Syr Gaw. introd. p. 12) says "both
Wace and La3. add that he (Gawain) was sent on

the embassy because he understood Latin"; but only Laȝ., not Wace, says this.

Laȝ. III, 48 (text B) Gaw. speaks a second time in answer to' the Roman emperor and associates himself with Arthur : —

"Belyn and Brenne, of wam we beop of-spronge."
and Laȝ. III, 52, as the Britans spring on their horses, Gaw. throws a defiance to the Romans — he will cut in pieces all pursuers etc.

Both of these speeches fail in Wace.
Wace II, 167 one of the Romans calls out: —

> ... ... "signor estés,
> Vilanie est que ne tornés."

and Gérin de Cartes turns and kills the Roman.

Cf. Laȝ. III, 54. Gawain is substituted for Gérin and Gérin's speech, combined with one which Wace gives Gawain further on in his combat with Marcel, is spoken by Gawain. This latter combat with Marcel is naturally omitted. Wace II, 171 Gawain kills a cousin of Marcel who has pursued him in the hope of vengeance. This also, for the same reason, fails in Laȝ.; but by making Gawain the first to resent the insult and by uniting the two battles Laȝ. has greatly emphasized Gawain's prowess.

Wace II, 177. Beof seizes the Roman commander Petreius, and thereby in great measure decides the fortune of the day.

Cf. Laȝ. III, 65—66. Beof does indeed throw Petreius to the ground, but it is Gawain whose bravery is praised, and who at length leads Petreius captive. Madden (ed. Laȝ. p. 400) has here remarked that Laȝ. varies from Wace with the intention of doing greater honour to Gaw. What Wace II, 178 says of Gawain's prowess Laȝ. has prefixed to this account.

Laȝ. III, 67 the prisoners are lead before Gawain and guarded during the night. This is not in Wace.

Laȝ. III, 105 calls Gaw. "swiðe stið imoded mon" but omits the praise of Gaw. and Howel which Wace has translated from Geof.; although Wace II, 210 corresponds to Laȝ. III, 107.

Wace II, 211, following Geof., gives a more detailed account of Gawain's fight with the emperor Lucius, but Laȝ. III, 108 has all the needful points.

Laȝ. III, 118—119, Gawain plays a very important part in Arthur's dream before the discovery of Modred's treachery. The dream is an addition of Laȝ.

Laȝ) III, 126. Arthur when he hears of Modred's
betrayal of his trust says that after chastising
him he will leave the kingdom to Gaw., his "mæie",
while he returns to Rome: —

"Þa stod hī up Walwain þat wes Arðures mæi,
And þas word saide, þe eorl wes abolȝe:
'Aldrihtē godd, domes waldend,
Al middel-ærdes mund, whi is hit wurðen,
Þat mi broðer Modred þis morð hafueð itimbred?
Ah to dæi ich at-sake hine here, biuoren þissere duȝeðe,
And ich hine for-demen wulle, mid drihtenes wille.
Mi seolf ich wulle hine an-hon haxst alre warien.
Þa quene ich wulle, mid goddes laȝe, al mid horsen
                                        [to-draȝe
For ne beo ich nauere bliðe, þe wile ich beoð aliue,
And þat ich habbe minne æm awræke mid þan bezste."

This passage fails entirely in Wace.

Finally Wace II, 223:

"Ocis i fu Gavains ses niés: —
Artus ot de lui dolor grant
Car il n'amoit nul home tant."
................................ʄ........

and again l. 13550: —

"Qui à Modred a grant haor
D'Aguisel a grant dol eu
Et de Gavain qu'il a perdu
Grans fu li dels de son neveu,
Li cors fist metre ne sai u."

Laȝ. III, 131 recounts, in. addition, Gawain's bravery in this same battle in which he was slain.

"Walwain bi-foren wende, and þene wæi rumde;
And sloh þer a-neuste peines elleouene.
He sloh Childriches sune, þe was þer mid his fader
[icume."

....

p. 132:—

ı "Þer wes Walwain aslæȝe, & idon of life daȝe
Þurh an eorle Sexisne. Særi wurde his saule.
Þa wes Arður særi, and sorhful an heort forþi;
And þas word bodede, ricchest alre Brutte:—
'Nu ich ileosed habbe mine sweines leofe.
    (text B has "Waweyn þat ich louede".)
Ich wuste bi mine sweuene whæt sorȝ in me weoren
[ȝeueðe.
I-slaȝen is Angel þe king, þe wes min aȝen deorling,
And Walwaine mi suster sune, Wa is me þat ich was
[mon iboren!"

            ı
The above comparison speaks for itself: in almost every instance Laȝamon varies from Wace in order to glorify Gawain.

(2.) *Robert Manning of Brune's translation
of Lantoft's chronicle.*

The part of Manning's chronicle which treats Arthur is unfortunately not published. It doubtless contains many English additions to Gawain's character.

Sir Fred. Madden quotes from the M.S. a few passages which are of interest:—

> "Sir Loth that wedded Anne,
> Wawan thei sone at Rome was than,
> To norise as the romance sais;
> He hight Wawan the *curtais*"

and again when Gaw. comes from Pope Sulpicius:—

> "Noble he was & *curteis*
> *Honour* of him men *rede* & *seis*."

Of the Roman Emperor's death (according to Madden translated from Lantoft, who was himself too good an Englishman to write correct French):—

> "I cannot say who did him falle;
> Bot Syr Wawayn said thei alle."

3.) *Arthur*
(ED. FURNIVALL E.E.T.S. 1864).

This is a short abstract of Arthur's career, containing only 640 lines. Gawain is only mentioned twice *l.* 564, his death, and *l.* 587:—

> "Waweynes body, as I reede,
> And other lordes þat weere deede,
> Arthour sente in-to Skotlonde,
> And buryed ham, y vnderstonde."

4.) *Morte Arthure*
(ED. PERRY E.E.T.S. FROM THORNTON M.S.),

probably written by Huchoun (cf. Trautmann, Anglia I.).

Gawain has here many of the surroundings, and traits which the romances of the 2nd class attribute to him.

Line 233:—

"Sir Gawayne þe worthye, Dame Waynour he hledys."

We shall find this association repeatedly.

In the battle with the Romans the bravery of "Sir Kayous" is emphasized. He appears, Class II, as Gawain's companion and foil.

Gawain's own delight in battle is repeatedly mentioned:—*l.* 259 his speech in praise of peace (cf. Wace and Laȝ.) is omitted; *l.* 2726 he is for attacking the enemy; *l.* 2752 he sneers at those who fight with words, and again *l.* 2820 he declares they have just enough to do to please them; 2853 he delights in the battle. In the three following instances the Morte Arthure agrees with Laȝ. where he differs from Geof. and Wace—*l.* 1342 Gawain speaks a second time before the Roman emperor; *l.* 1369 he slays the foremost of the pursuers and *l.* 3725 ff. gives the details of Gawain's last battle; this Laȝ. has only outlined.

Gawain's speech to the conquered Priamus, *l.* 2645:—

"Gruche noghte, gude syr, þofe me this grace happene;
It es þe gifte of Gode, the gree es hys awene."

strikes the oft repeated sententious tone.

In no other romance is the praise of Gaw.
more splendid cf. *l.* 3876, Modred speaks:—

"He was makles one molde, nane be my trowhe;
This was syr Gawayne the gude, þe gladdeste of othire,
And the graciouseste gome that undire God lyffede,
Nane hardyeste of hande, happyeste in armes,
And the hendeste in hawle undire hevene riche."

Arthur weeps over Gawain's dead body and
says *l.* 3965:—

"Þou was worthy to be the kynge thofe I þe corowne
[bare.
My wele & my wirchipe of alle þis werlde riche
Was wonnene thourghe syr Gawayne, & thourghe his
[witte one."

II. ROMANCES WHICH BELONG TO
THE LATER DEVELOPMENT OF THE ARTHUR-SAGA,

and which treat occurrences supposed to take place
during the twelve years' peace.

Compare M. Gaston Paris in the Romania for
October 1881. (He has been speaking of the bio-
graphical poems.) "Dans la même classe que les
romans biographiques il faut placer les romans épisodiques racontant quelque exploit isolé d'un chevalier
célèbre; presque tous les romans de ce genre sont
consacrés à Gauvain."

The following Gawain romances are English "romans épisodiques". I arrange them, according to their known sources, in three divisions.

A. Romances which show a more original treatment of the Arthur-saga.

B. Romances founded upon the romances of Crestien de Troies.

C. Romances which are based upon other French romances.

A.

There are only four romances or ballads in this class.

I. Anturs of Arther at the Tarnewalhelan.

(ED. MADDEN "SYR GAW." 1839 AND ROBSON "THREE METRICAL ROMANCES" FOR THE CAMDEN SOC. 1842.)

The whole of this quaint and excellent romance is a glorification of Gawain.

Gaw.'s friendship for Guinevere and hers for him is emphasized—the poem opens with the description of a hunt, Gaw. waits on the queen; stanza VI he remains with her while the others—Cador, Clegius, Costantyne and Cay take flight; st. VII when the ghost appears "he cumforthes the quene

6

throghe his kny3thed" and "went to it in haste,"
"afraid was he never yet;" before Gaw.'s encounter
with the strange knight:—

> "And thenne Dame Gaynour grette
> For Gauan the gode;"

when he is wounded:—"Gaynor grette for his sake;"
she begs Arthur to make peace.

Before this same fight with Galrun Arthur
says:—

> "I wold notte for no lordscip se thi life lorne"
> 'Lette go', cothe Sir Gauan, God stond with the ry3te"

and again when he is wounded Arthur is "hurt in
heart."

Gawain naturally conquers. Arthur bestows lands
upon him and Gawain in his turn generously enriches
the conquered Galrun.

Ten Brink (Engl. Lit. p. 421) says, in speaking
of this romance:—"dabei ahnt man eine mehr direct
praktische tendenz, und man ist versucht zu fragen, wen
der dichter unter Gawein, der den mittelpunkt des
ganzen bildet, hat darstellen wollen." Gawain's
character, however, seems completely in accordance
with that given him in the following romances—his
bravery, and generosity, and the king's and queen's

love toward him, while the praises bestowed upon him by the poet are even surpassed by those in Golagrus and Gawain.

II. *The Avowynge of King Arther, Sir Gawan, Sir Kaye, and Sir Bawdewyn of Bretan.*

(ED. ROBSON 1842).

Here, as often, we see Gawain, Kay, and Bawdewyn associated together.

Gaw.'s friendship for Kay and the opposition of his courtesy to Kay's discourtesy:—stanza XXIV Gaw. ransoms Kay by fighting with and conquering Menealfe; st. XXVIII when Kay scoffs at the fallen knight:—

> "Thenne speke Gauan to Kay,
> A mon's happe is not ay,
> Is none so sekur of a say
> Butte he may harmes hente."

and st. XXIX he again reproves Kay:—

> "And Gauan sayd, 'God forbede!
> For he is duȝti in dede' —
> Prayes the knyȝte gud spede
> To take hit none ille,
> If Kay speke wurdes kene."

There is the same relation between Gaw. and Guinevere:—Gaw. sends Menealfe to Gaynour

from "Gawan hur knight"; st. xxxvi Guinevere
says :—

       — — — — "God almyȝti
       Saue me Gawan, my knyȝte,
       That thus for wemen con fiȝte,
       Tw wothus him were".

There is the same love between Arthur and
Gaw. and the same eulogy of Gaw.:—st. xxxiv

       "Grete God', quod the king,
       'Gif Gawan gode endinge,
       For he is sekur in alle kynne thinge,
       To cowuntur with a knyȝte!
       Of alle playus he berus the prise
       Lovs of ther ladise."

IIIa. Fragment of the marriaye of Sir Gawaine.
b. The Weddynge of Sir Gawen and Dame Ragnell.
(ED. MADDEN FROM PERCY M. S. "SYR GAW. etc.").

These are two different versions of the same
story. The same motive appears as in the Anturs
of Arther at the *Tarnewalhelan.* (Arthur also rides
to *Tearne-wadling*). Arthur has aroused the enmity
of a strange knight by giving his lands to Gawain;
he must therefore either lose his life or tell "what
thing women love best in feld and town." Gawain
gives the greatest proof of his devotion to Arthur
by his marriage to the woman described below who,

on that condition alone, consents to solve the riddle
and thus save Arthur's life.

After the marriage she asks him whether he
will have her fair by night ·or by day and Gaw.
proves his courtesy by leaving her the choice;
Weddynge of Gaw. *l.* 879 she says: —

"Gode thanke hyme of his curtesye,
He savide me frome chaunce ande vilony".

There is the usual opposition of Kay and Gaw.:
Kay (Frag. of marriage of Gaw.) scoffs at the
hideous lady: "whosœuer kisses this lady"..........
"of his kiss he stands in feare," *l.* 136 "Peace coz
Kay', then said sir Gawaine."

This same story is found in the Gesta
Romanorum, in Gower's Confessio Amantis, and in
the Wife of Bath's tale; but in the elaboration of
what is peculiar to these two ballads I think we
can recognize traces of Crestien's Perceval. It is
the more probable, as this romance (cf. cl. B. p.
87 ff.) has had such a paramount influence upon
the other Gawain-romances.

Weddynge of Gaw.: *l.* 228 ff.:—

"Ande ther he mette withe a lady:—
She was as vngoodly a creature,
As euer mane sawe, witheoute mesure.
....

Her face was rede, her nose snotyde with alle,
Her mowithe wyde, *her tethe yalowe ouer alle,*
Withe bleryde eyene gretter thene a balle,
Her mowithe was nott to lake;
Her tethe hyng ouer her lyppe,
Her chekys syde as wemen's hyppe,
A lute she bare vpon her bake,
Her neke long ande therto greatt,
Her *here cloteryd one ane hepe,*
In sholders she was a *yarde brode.*
Hangyng pappys to be ane hors-lode.
Ande *lyke a barelle* she was made.

. . . .

She satt one a palfray was gay begone,
Withe gold besett, and many a precious stone.
Ther was ane vnsemely syght,
So fowlle a creature, witheoute measure
To ryde so gayly, I you ensure."

and *l.* 549:—

"She had 2 *tethe* on euery syde
As *borys tuske,* I wolle nott hyde,
Of lengthe a large *handfulle.*"

It will be seen by comparing the above lines
with Crestien's description of "la damoisele hydeuse"
Perc. *l.* 5998 ff. that there is a striking similarity
between the two. Part of the French description
was quoted page 63; I am at present unable to
obtain the ed. of Perceval. Cf. however Wolfram's
Parzival (ed. Lachm.) book VI, page 153—155

where he also paraphrases Crestien's description and
especially :—

> *"Zwên ebers zene* ir für den munt
> Giengen wol *spannen* lanc."

The continuation of Crestien's Perceval contains
a similar description, likewise modelled upon that of
"la damoisele hydeuse." Here as in the English
romance Kay scoffs at her ugliness. It is probable
that both descriptions influenced the details of our
story. If this be so these two romances form a fit
transition to class B.

B.

ROMANCES FOUNDED UPON CRESTIEN DE TROIES.

I. THOSE BASED UPON LE ROMAN DE PERCEVAL.

1. *The Knightly Tale of Golagros and Gawane.*
(ED. MADDEN "SYR GAW. etc.", AND TRAUTMANN ANGLIA II).

Madden first pointed out that this romance was
put together out of two episodes in Perceval—Kay's
adventure with the dwarf and the peacock, and Castel
Orgueillos. In part first Kay's discourtesy and
Gawain's courtesy are opposed. In part second
Gawain after conquering in a valiantly contested

battle allows himself to appear to be taken captive out
of courtesy toward the fallen knight and his amie.

The romance abounds in extragant praise of Gaw.
Cf. 118:—

"Schir Gawane the gay, gratius & gude,
Schur ye knaw that schir Kay is crabbit of kynde."
Cf. Gaw. *l.* 393:—

"Egir, & ertand, and ryght anterus,
Illuminat vith lawte, & vith lufe lasit."
and *l.* 804 ff.:—

"Sen ye ar sa wourschipfulle & wourthy in were,
Demyt with the derrest, maist doughly in deid."
Line 389:—

"Than schir Gawayne the gay, gude, & gracius,
That ever wes beildit in blis & bounte embrasit
Joly & gentill, & full cheuailrus
That neuer poynt of his prise wes funden defasit."

Line 1135, as Gaw. is thought to be taken
prisoner:

"The flour of knighthede is caught throu his cruelty!
Now is pe Round Tabul rebutit, richest of rent,
Quhen wourshipful Wawane, pe wit of our were
Is led to ane presoune.
Now failyeis gude fortune."

2 a. *Sir Gawayne and the Green Knight* (ED. MADDEN,
AND MORRIS),

This, as has been shown part II, is composed
chiefly of two adventures in Perceval. While preserv-

ing the spirit of the other romances the poet has given Gaw.'s character a freshness and originality which is doubly charming after the stereotyped model Knight we meet elsewhere.

The romance contains some of the most graceful praise of Gaw. e. g. *l.* 914 ff. :—

> "By-fore alle men vpon molde, his mensk is þe most.
> Vch segge ful softly sayde to his fere,
> Non schal we semlych se sleȝteȝ of peweȝ,
> And þe teccheles termes of talkyng noble."

Line 109 :—

> "There gode Gawan watȝ grayped, Gwenore bisyde."

Line 1012 :—

> "Bischop Bawdewyn abof bi-gineȝ þe table".

2 b. The Ballad of the Green Knight (ED. MADDEN "BYR GAW. etc.")

This is a ballad version of Sir Gaw. and the Green Knight. The motives are simplified. Gaw. has lost all indivuality and appears with his epitheton of "curteous". The Green Knight is named Syr Bredbeddle. His wife loved Sir Gaw. secretly and her mother Aggteb, the witch, sent her son-in-law after Gaw. because "Sir Gawane was bold and handye and thereto full of curtesye"; *l.*

439:—Sir Gaw. "soe curteous and free;" Sir Bredbeddle addresses Gaw. *l.* 483:—

> "The gentlest knight in this land,
> Men told me of great renowne
> Of curtesie. thou might have won the crowne
> Above free and bound,
> And alsœ of great gentrye."

2 c. *The Turke and Gowin* (ED. MADDEN).

According to Madden this is founded upon a
version of the Green Knight. Line 153 "Bishopp Sir
Bodwine" is mentioned.

2 d. *Fragment of the Ballad of King Arthur and the King of Cornwall* (ED. MADDEN).

This ballad, being only a fragment, is difficult
to place; it seems to be connected with the Green
Knight series by Sir Bredbeddle, who is also called
the "Green Knight". He conjures with the aid of
his "little book", and says he will encounter the
"lodly feend" with his "collen brand, Millaine knife
and *danish axe.*"

3. *The Jeast of Syr Gawayne* (ED. MADDEN).

The whole story is taken out of Perceval,
being Gaw's adventure with the sister of Brandalis.
Concerning Gaw. nothing of interest is added.

4. *Sir Perceval of Galles* (ED. HALLIWELL, "THORNTON ROMANCES" 1844).

This is a very rough, popular romance put together out of different adventures of Perceval related by Crestien. The beginning of the Engl. Perceval follows the French more exactly; even here however there are a number of coarse additions, e. g. Perceval *burns* the body of the red knight and, meeting the red knight's mother, flings her also into the flames.

Known names are substituted for the less familiar ones of the French romance. Ewayne, instead of Bawdewyn, is the companion of Gaw. and Kay. It is interesting to note the prominence of Gaw.; Ewayne, *l.* 262 "Gawayne with honour," and Kay are substituted for the three knights whom Perceval meets in the forest; in the description of the tournament *l.* 1390:—

> „Another Ewayne the floure,
> The thirde Wawayne with honoure,
> And Kay the kene knyghte."

l. 513 Gaw. recognizes Perceval at Arthur's court and speaks kindly to him; *l.* 765 Gaw. is substituted for the squire in Crestien, he follows after "for the child's sake" and unlaces the armour of the Red Knight and arms Perceval.

Gaw.'s courtesy and Kay's discourtesy:—to Perceval's question if the three knights were angels:—

l. 285:—

> "Bot thanne ansuerde syr Gawayne,
> Faire and courtaisely agayne."

l. 291:—

> "To Gawayne that was meke & mylde
> And softe of ansuare."

l. 305:—He reproves Kay for his rough answer.

l. 1261 ff. is striking as showing Gaw. labelled with his chief virtue:—

> "Scho calde appone hir chaymbirlayne
> Was called hende Hatlayne,
> The curtasye of Wawayne,
>   He weldis in wane."

II. ROMANCES BASED ON OTHER WORKS OF CRESTIEN.

There is only one which concerns Gawain.

Gawain and Ywayne (ED. RITSON, "ANCIENT ENGLISH METRICAL ROMANCES," VOL. I).

I have compared this romance with Crestien's "Chevalier au Lyon", and the result has proved that the English translator has added nothing to Gawain's character; in almost every case where he is mentioned the English renders the French words.

I have noted a few slight differences: —
p. 66: —

"A thowsand sithes welkum sho says
And so es sir Gawayne the *curtayse*,"

where Crestien has "sire Gauvains, ses niés."

"Thai (Gaw. & Ywayne) war doghty both in fer
Thai wan the prise both fer & ner."

where Crestien has nothing corresponding.

p. 68: — " gude Gawaye" renders "mon seignor
Gauvain".

p. 154: — "Sir Gawayn answered als curtays"
translates "mes sire Gauvains li douz."

Ywayne's speech at the close of the duel between
him and Gaw. shows the manner in which Gaw. is
praised in this romance: —

— — — — — "I hat Ywayne,
That lufes the more by se and sand,
Than any man that is lifand,
For mani dedes that thou me did,
And curtaysi ye have me kyd."

III. THOSE DRAWN FROM OTHER FRENCH SOURCES.

(*The Squyr of Lowe Degre*, Ritson III, belongs
here, but I am at present unable to obtain the
romance.)

1. *Launfal* (ED. RITSON).

This is a translation of one of the *lais* of Marie de France. Although I have not been able to obtain the original *lai* for comparison, I will quote a few passages which are so entirely in the spirit of the Engl. poems that they may easily be additions of the translator.

Line 13 "Gawain and Perseval" are mentioned together; *l.* 813:—

> "noble knyghtes twayn
> syr Perceval & syr Gawayn"

go bail for Launfal.

Gaw.'s friendship for Launfal is emphasized:—line 892 he is the first to comfort Launfal:— ·

> "Tho seyde Gaweyn, that curtayse knyght,
> Launfal, her cometh thy swete wyght."

and again:—

> "Tho seyde Gawayn, that corteys knyght,
> Launfal brodyr drede the no wyght,"

and Launfal answers:—

> "Gaweyn my lefly frende."

Gaw. is near the queen 661:—

> "The quene yede to the formeste ende,
> Betwene Launfal & Gauweyn the hende,
> And after her ladyes bryght."

2. *Lybeas* (ED. RITSON).

There is the same association of Gawain and Perceval:—*l.* 178, when Elene is given the inexperienced Lybeas as her champion, she says:—

> (thou) "hast knyghtes of mayn,
> Lancelot, Perceval & Gaweyn
> Prys in ech turnement."

l. 218 speaking of the knights who arm Lybeas:—

> "The firste was syr Gaweyn,
> That other syr Percevale,
> And Eweyn, and Agrafrayn."

Of Gaw.'s valour:—

l. 1644:—

> "Ne sygh y come her before
> So redy a knyght to my pay.
> A thoghth y have myn herte wythinne
> That thou art com of Gawenys kynne,
> That ys so stout & gay."

A lady is turned into a "worm" till she:—

> "had kyste Gaweyn
> Eyther som other knyght sertayn
> That wer of hys hende."

3 a. *Syre Gawene and the Carle of Carelyle* (ED. MADDEN, "SYR GAW." etc.)

According to Madden the story is taken from "Le Chevalier à l'Epée".

Gaw., Kay and "Byschope Bawdewynne" come
to the Carle of Carelyle's castle, *l.* 127 Gaw. is
called "gentille"; *l.* 184 he asks courteously for lodg-
ing. During the entertainment Kay, Bawdewynne
and Gaw. go out to care for their steeds; the
former two drive away the Carle's foal to make place
for their own steeds, but Gaw. covers the foal with
his green mantle and cares for it like his own charger.
At the evening meal the Carle forces Gaw. to strike
him with a spear; he then seats him by his wife
with whom Gaw. falls in love. When they retire
for the night the Carle allows Gaw. to kiss his wife
watching him narrowly all the while; he then com-
mends him to his daughter's courtesy whom he gives
him in marriage on the following day. Beyond the
story there is no verbal praise of Gaw.

Syr Raynbrowne, "the knyзt of armus grene"
is mentioned in this romance.

3 b. *Carle off Carlile* (ED. MADDEN).

In this later version of the older romance,
just as in the Ballad of the Green Knight, Gawain's
courtesy is his one virtue; also „Byschope Bawdewynne" reappears as "Bishop Bodwin" just as
"Bischop Bawdewyn" of Sir Gaw. and the Gr. Kn.

becomes "Bishopp sir Bodwine" in the Turke and Gowin. Line 30:—

"Hie (Gaw.) was the curteous knight amongst them all."

l. 135 (Gaw.):

"Curteously on the gates dange."

l. 137:—

"Gawaine answered him curteously."

l. 155:—

"Then answered Gawaine that was curteous aye."

l. 288 (The Carle):—

"thanked him of his curtesye."

l. 335 the Carle leads him to his wife's room and says:—

"Gawaine of curtesye get into bed."

l. 373:—

"Sir Gawaine courteous & kind."

l. 37:—

"& Ironside as I weene
Gate the knight of armour greene
Certes as I understand
Of a faire lady of Blaunchland."

There may be noted the following interconnection of persons and incidents not found elsewhere. (Madden has suggested that the Archbishop of Canterbury Baldwin who held the see from 1184—1191 may have been substitued for Dubricius. This Baldwin

7

is also mentioned in the romance of Richard Cœur de Lion.)

Bishop Bawdewyn.	Green Knight.	Gaw. strikes off a head.	Gaw. tempted by a lady.
Sir Gaw. & Gr. Kn. (Bawdewyn)	Sir Gaw. & Gr. Kn. ("Bernlak de Hautdesert")	Sir Gaw. & Gr. Kn.	Sir Gaw. & Gr. Kn.
Carle of Carelyle (Bawdewyne)	Ballad of Gr. Kn. (Sir Bredbeddle)	Ballad of Gr. Kn.	Ballad of Gr. Kn.
Carle off Carlile (Sir Bodwin)	Carle of Carelyle (Sir Reynbroune)	Carle of Carelyle	Carle of Carelyle
Turke & Gowin (Sir Bodwine)	Carle off Carlile ("Knight of armes grene")	Carle off Carlile	Carle off Carlile
Avow. of Ar., Gaw. etc. (Sir Bowdewyn)	King of Cornwall (Sir Bredbedle, conjurer, with "danlsb axe".)	Turke & Gowin	

As containing notices of Gawain, *Tristram* (ed. Sir Walter Scott) belongs here, as do also the rhymed *Arthur and Merlin, Lancelot* and one or two other romances. I have not been able to obtain the Tristram, and the other romances are excluded because, without a comparison with the originals, which were inaccessible, it is impossible to decide what is *English* :— for these and for the prose romances, which lie outside my subject, compare Sir Fred. Madden's Syr Gaw. legend.

GAWAIN IN OTHER POEMS,
NOT BELONGING TO THE LEGENDS OF THE ROUND TABLE.

I will re-quote Madden's collection of lines, which, although I have read through a number of romances for the purpose, I have not been able to enlarge.

In prefatory lines to Collection of metrial legends of the saints :—

"Of Roulond & of Olyuere & Guy of Warwyk,
Of Wawayne & Tristram that ne founde here ylike."

Richard Cœur de Lyon (ed. Weber II):—

"Off King Arthour and off Gawayn."

Owl and Nightingale :—

"I take witness of Sire Wawain."

Cursor Mundi :—

> "As Wawan, Cai & other stabell
> Were to were the Ronde Tabell."

Chaucer, Rom. of the Rose 2209 ff., and Squyeres Tale *l.* 87 :—

> "Than Gaweyn with his olde curtesye
> They he were come ayein out of fayrye
> Ne couthe him nought amende with no word."

Metrical version of Guido de Colonna's war of Troye :—

> "Off Bevis, Guy & of Wawayn."

Sir Degrevant (ed. Halliwell "Thornton Rom.") *l.* 23 :—

> "He was known for kene,
> Wyth Persevalle & Gawayne."

Madden has suggested that Spenser's portrait of Sir Calidore in the sixth book of the Fairy Queen is moddled upon Gawain; undoubtedly Calidore's character is in exact accordance with that of Gawain in English poems.

The various quotations make clear to us especially the following traits in the English conception of Gawain.

(1) *His constant association with Guinevere.*

These romances make no reference to her love for Lancelot. Gawain waits on her and serves her

in his character of the most courteous and well born
of all the knights of Arthur's table.

Cf. I, 3. Morte Arthure. He leads Guinevere to table.

II A, 1. Anturs of Arthur. He waits on her during the hunt;
[she weeps when he is wounded.

II A, 2. Avow. of Art. Gaw. etc.—He sends Menealfe to
[Guinevere from "Gaw. hur knight", and she praises him.

II B, 2. Sir Gaw. and the Gr. Kn. He sits beside Guin.
[at the feast.

II C, 1. Launfal: "The quene yede to the formeste ende
Betweene Launfal & Gaweyn the hende."

②) *His friendship for his brother knights.*

II A, 2. Avow. of Art. Gaw. etc. He pays Kay's ransom.
II B, I, 4. Perceval of Galles. His friendship for Perceval.
II B, II, 1. Gaw. and Ywayne. His friendship for Ywayne.
II C, 1. Launfal. His friendship for Launfal.

③ *His association with Perceval.*

This is probably due to the popularity of the ·
Roman de Perceval in which Gaw. and Perc. are
equally celebrated.

II B, 4. Perceval of Galles.
II C, 1. Launfal.
II C, 2. Lybeas.
Sir Degrevant.

④.) *His courtesy.*

This is so emphasized every where that it is
impossible to enumerate all the notices. As a rule

the later the romance the greater the prominence of this stereotyped virtue. Cf. the later version of Sir Gaw. and the Gr. Kn. and the Carle of Carelyle.

(5.) *His opposition to the discourteous Kay.*

II A, 2.   Avow. of Art., Gaw. etc.
II B, 1.   Gol. and Gaw.
II A, 3, a. The Marriage of Gaw.
II B, 4.   Perceval of Galles.
II C, 3, a. Syre Gaw. & the Carle of Carelyle, & b. Carle
                                    [off Carlile.

(6) *The love existing between him and Arthur.*

I, 1. La3amon repeatedly emphasizes this love
I, 3. Morte Arthure. Arthur's lament over Gaw. is one of
     [the strongest testimonies to his devotion to Gaw.
II A, 2.   Avow. of Art. Gaw. etc., cf. Arthur's speech.
II A, 3, a. Marriage of Gaw. & b. Weddynge of Gaw. he
                      [interposes to save Arthur's life.
II B, 2.   Sir Gaw. & the Gr. Kn. He also interposes
                      [between Arthur & danger.

Apart from the above traits, his nobility, his generosity, his prowess, his truth are praised. No breath of discredit touches Gawain in this class of romances.

For the sake of the direct contrast, I quote the following passages:—the only ones in the Idyls of the King in which Gawain is characterized. Since most English-speaking people derive from these poems of Mr. Tennyson their whole acquaintance with the Round Table it will be seen that their Gawain, except for a varnish of gentle manners, is entirely dissimilar to the hero of their ancestors. Mr. Tennyson has followed the most unfavourable of the later French romances.

The Coming of Arthur (Tauchnitz ed. vol. VI, p. 19 ff.) contains the first introduction of Gaw.:

> "And Gawain went and breaking into song
> Sprang out and followed by his flying hair
> Ran like a colt and leapt at all he saw."

Gareth and Lynette, Enid, (upon re-reading this best constructed of all the Idyls I find it is little more than a translation of Crestien's Erec.), and *Vivien* scarcely mention Gawain.

Elaine (vol. I, p. 133): —

> "To this the courteous Prince
> Accorded with his wonted courtesy,
> Courtesy with a touch of traitor in it."

He makes love to Elaine and gives her the jewels Arthur had commissioned him to bestow upon Lancelot only. Arthur says p. 136: —

> "Too courteous truly! you shall go no more
> On quest of mine, seeing that you forget
> Obedience is the courtesy due to kings."

The Grail (vol. VI)

Arthur speaks, p. 77:—

> "Gawain was this Quest for thee?'
> 'Nay lord', said Gawain, 'not for such as I,
> Therefore I communed with a saintly man,
> Who made me sure the Quest was not for me
> For I was much awearied of the Quest;
> But found a silken pavilion in a field,
> And merry maidens in it; and then this gale
> Tore my pavilion from the tenting-pin,
> And blew my merry maidens all about
> With all discomfort, yea, and but for this,
> My twelvemonth and a day were pleasant to me."

p. 84:—

> "The hall long silent till Sir Gawain — nay,
> Brother I need not tell thee — foolish words —
> ....
> A reckless and irreverent knight was he."

Peleas and Etàrre (vol. VI, 117)

Peleas trusts Gawain by whom he is basely deceived; he says:—

> „Alas that ever knight should be so false!"

Guinevere contains nothing.

The Last Tournament:—

> "Dagonet, the fool, whom Gawain in his mood
> Had made mock knight of Arthur's Table Round."

The Passing of Arthur (vol. VI, 131—133):—

> "Before that last wierd battle in the west
> There came on Arthur sleeping, Gawain killed
> In Lancelot's war, the ghost of Gawain blown
> Along a wandering wind, and past his ear
> Went shrilling 'Hollow, hollow all delight!'"

Sir Bedevere says:—

> "Light was Gawain in life, and light in death
> Is Gawain for the ghost is as the man."